An Alcoholic in the Family

An Alcoholic in the Family

MARY BURTON

FABER AND FABER
3 Queen Square
London

First published in 1974
by Faber and Faber Limited
3 Queen Square London WC1
Printed in Great Britain by
Latimer Trend & Company Ltd Plymouth

ISBN 0 571 10355 3

I dedicate this book to all my friends who, wittingly or unwittingly, helped me to live it, in the confidence that they will not break my anonymity.

Chapter One

LOOKING BACK twenty-four years, I can see now that I must have had a clear picture, at eighteen, of the sort of man I intended to marry. He would be intelligent, and cultured, working preferably in a profession though I would not insist on that provided he was not too materialistic. He would share with me his interests and never hide any part of his life from me for my marriage must be a partnership, not a lord and vassal arrangement. With a very modest educational achievement behind me at school, I nevertheless had stirrings from time to time of intellectual interest. I had acquired a delight in music, though painting and poetry were joys which I did not comprehend; I read reasonable literature, though apart from a devotion to Shakespeare at the Old Vic, I ventured little into the classics. With a family background which was unacquisitive, I had no strong desire for the extravagant pleasures and I held a firmly instilled belief in the value of work and its relation to the achievement of happiness.

When I sought a job, it was its intrinsic interest to me that I regarded as of prime importance rather than its financial reward, though I was happy to be considered worth a rise in salary. I had enjoyed the pleasures of some of the smart London restaurants and the flattering sensation of importance which the attentiveness of a posse of obsequious waiters gave me when I was taken out by the better-off of my boy-friends, but after one or two visits to night-clubs I decided that they were rather boring. I found far more enjoyment in standing in the promenade at the Royal Albert Hall which, although it did not give me that same elevated sense of having reached the heights of society life which my only visit to Churchill's night-club brought, neither caused me to wake up the next morning with a hangover. I have a very clear memory of my only real humdinger of a hangover. There were three girls in my family, and we were each expected to take our turn in cooking the Sunday lunch. After one dizzy Saturday night, it was my turn to produce the meal for our family of six. My mother, a very practical woman with a strongly developed appreciation of right and wrong and no hesitation in clearly expressing her views and disapprobation of those who contravened them, kept popping in and out of the kitchen. It was a hell of a morning. One moment I was sitting nursing my pounding head in my hands among the clutter of crocks and ingredients on the kitchen table, the next I had, at the sound of her bright footsteps clipping along the passage, jerked myself to my feet with a sickening lurch to be found energetically beating the batter for the Yorkshire pudding, gay conversation bubbling unconvincingly from my lips. I learnt very early how to dissimulate in order to avoid painful confrontation, and this was an acquirement for which subsequently, in my married life, I found constant use.

In adolescence, I had formed very clear and decided views about life and morality—about my life and my morality—which, though they were certainly shaped by environmental pressures and undermined by a conscience well established in childhood that caused doubt and uncertainty at surface level, have helped me through more difficulties and crises than they have caused. I believed that the worst sin in the world is intentionally to hurt another person. I believed that all the other sins are towards oneself and that, so long as no hurt is caused, conventions and established standards all require questioning and not a placid or resentful acquiescence. This early decision on how I felt it necessary to behave brought about a certain resistance on my part against taking advice and this may have caused me to go to extremes of disagreement which worried my parents, but since they could not know that I held, for myself, a very strongly defined code of morality and that my behaviour was based on a practical exercise of that code, their need for worry was more imagined than real. The snag was my ability to wear a false face, which perhaps implied more than it disguised.

When I met John, I was a self-confident young woman of eighteen, grown out of a professional middle-class, stable family without much money but happy, who had mixed very much with her own kind, more ready to be dazzled by intellectual than material success but regarding both as probably beyond her reach and not particularly concerned anyway. An early physical maturer, I had had my fair share of boy-friends; a competent secretary, I took pleasure in my job and glowed in the satisfaction of knowing that I was appreciated; protected by my environment and a selfishness derived from my early sense of identity and self-assertion, I had very little perception of sensitivity and uncertainty in others.

John was a little older than my other suitors, not much but enough to make me feel he had seen more of life. He was tall and thin, with a slight, scarcely perceptible stoop. He had the coarse, fair curly hair which feels springy to the touch and is generally not so prone to early sparseness as softer fine hair. His blue eyes were set deep and there was a cragginess about the bone around the sockets which I associated with the toughness of a north country miner, and already, while he was yet in his mid twenties, crinkle lines of laughter were etched from their outer corners. His mouth was well defined, thin yet not mean, and curled attractively at the edges. I wondered what it would feel like to be kissed by that mouth and imagined that there would be a delightful firmness about it; I soon discovered that I was right. I noticed that he occasionally stammered, particularly when instructing a taxi driver or ordering from a waiter, as though authority made him uneasy, and I had to restrain myself from taking over from him. He later told me that he had had, as a child, to attend a clinic for a course of speech therapy because his stutter was so bad. It rarely appeared now and when it did I found it rather endearing.

When I met John in 1948 he had recently been demobilised from his army service, which had begun at the tail end of the war, with the rank of Captain. He did not live locally, so I knew nothing of his background, but his accent was acceptable, slightly public school; I was a snob and would not have gone out with a working-class boy. Although, put baldly, this sounds unpleasant and prejudiced, I believe my attitude was rooted in the fair and realistic observation that it is easier to live with another person who has derived from the same type of background as oneself; there is so much that we accept without question which, for somebody from a different background or upbringing, is magnified out of proportion to its importance and so creates a peculiar sensibility which, if suppressed, causes misunderstanding and tension. Where differences in values and attitudes are recognised and openly acknowledged it is possible to overcome them; where they are denied, they fester and become a canker of resentment.

I had no pretensions to a superior ancestry myself. My mother came from a lower middle-class family who had been shopkeepers in the East End of London; my paternal grandfather had been a butler. All but my maternal grandfather died before I was born and he died when I was ten years old. So, although I vaguely knew the family background, I had had little direct contact with it. My own upbringing had been firmly middle class, my father earning his living as a freelance technical journalist for as long as I could remember. He had, in his quiet, unpretentious way, pulled himself up in the world but without the aggressive self-assertion that sometimes characterises the man who achieves an upward social mobility. He is a gentle man, and I rarely heard him raise his voice in anger. His strongest expletive was 'Blimey', and he has a deeply ingrained care for good manners and an enormous respect for traditional values and for learning. He would never be seen in braces and took great pride in keeping the shoes of the whole family well burnished, for slovenliness was offensive to him. I suppose both the love of tradition and of the external niceties of living were taught to him by his father, and I have inherited from him my more recently discovered delight in study and learning along with my early snob instincts. Neither of us despise people with different modes of living from our own, we simply feel uncomfortable with them; the loss is ours, of course, for we are confined by our intolerance. My father, despite the fact that he associated with the world of commerce in his profession as a journalist, has the air and dignity of a man dealing in less mundane matters. I think he would have enjoyed a career in a more academic world.

It was eighteen months before John invited me home although he had stayed frequently with my family. By this time we were very much in love. He had read far more widely than I, he talked entertainingly and was sometimes witty, and we both enjoyed going to concerts. We both worked in the same firm and I was encouraging him to enter a professional career. He did, I admit, show a regrettable tendency to dismiss my attempts to make him think seriously of his future, and I did not very much like his inclination to make straight for the nearest pub whenever we met before we started the evening, or even to make that the evening. He was always short of money and our courtship was pursued a lot of the time in pubs and museums. My mother noted John's habit of telephoning me, on the evenings we did not meet, after the pubs had closed, but she also expressed the opinion that he had the eyes of a poet or a fanatic and this appealed to me. I chose to ignore her remarks about his drinking habits, putting these down to what I considered was her general intolerance of people with different standards from herself, and treasured a romantic notion of the talented poetic genius whom I was going to inspire.

When he finally took me home to meet his family, I was aghast though with my accustomed aplomb I tried not to show it. They lived in a council house in a row of terraced council houses, and his father, though I believe he wore a collar and tie for my visit, was obviously a man who took his ease in his shirtsleeves and braces. I remember the occasion as very stiff and difficult. For a few days after the visit, I was in a state of confusion. I had planned, as my future parents-in-law, a couple modelled on some friends of my parents and was not sure that I could accept such a totally unlike pair. John sensed that something was wrong and I suppose that he must have known the reason for my sudden change in manner, but neither of us mentioned the cause, only the effect. 'Crumbs, darling,' he said, as we walked through St. James's Park one evening, 'don't you love me any more?' My future poetic genius was as dumbfounded as I was. I assured him that I did love him, my renewed fervour compounded of shame at my own behaviour as well as the intense physical attraction that he held for me.

And so we were married, in the spring of 1952, after an eighteen-month engagement, and for a while we caught the same train to London in the morning and met at the barrier in the evening as excited by each other's company as any other newly married couple. When autumn came, and the beginning of the academic year, John enrolled in an evening class in preparation for his entry into apprenticeship with a professional firm. I recall the winter evenings when, having completed the domestic tasks in our flat, after my own return from London, I would walk the dog down to the station to meet him off his train. I remember how I would arrive just in time to see the passengers trickling through the barrier and, with dog straining at the leash, stand expectant in the anticipated joy of welcoming my loved husband, his face creased in the familiar smile of recognition and embracing warmth which shut everybody out from our private happiness and absorption with each other. He had an ancient sand-coloured coat which enveloped him like an oversized dressing-gown, and together we would walk up the hill to home, after the first tingling contact of our faces pressed together in the frosty night air, my cold hand clasped in his warm one thrust deep into his torn pocket against the lovely moulded hardness of his thigh. I would chatter of my day, usually spilling over in my desire to include him in my enthusiasms. I remember, too, how sometimes he would not appear at the barrier and how Charley, the old ticket collector who had worked at the station for as long as I could remember, would let me sit on the stool behind him in his wooden box, the dog crouched in the corner, and share his tiny electric fire against the cold of the night until the next train from London arrived. Because I had Charley to gossip with, I did not have a chance to work up any resentment against John for not letting me know he had missed the train. I sometimes suggested that he could have telephoned me, but he always had the ready answer that the class had gone on a bit late and he had not had time, and I did not care to spoil the pleasure of being with him by pressing the point, even though he often smelt of beer. In that cold air, it added to the warmth of his nearness and already, perhaps, was becoming too familiar a part of his presence to be distinguishable from the redolence of pipe tobacco and general maleness. There was one occasion when he did not arrive on the second train either, and I walked home with the dog, feeling a tiny seed of doubt, an uncomfortable sensation that the need I had for him was, perhaps, stronger than the need he had for me, that there might be a part of his life which he chose not to share with me. There was a telephone call when I got home; he was in Charing Cross Hospital, having been seized with an uncontrollable nose-bleed caused by a fall down some steps as he left his class, and was being treated.

The nose-bleeds became common as the years progressed. John had suffered a bang on the bridge of his nose in childhood and I believed that they must be caused by some remaining weakness. He himself gave me the most extraordinary reason for the sudden attacks: he had been told that it was because he did not wear a hat. We had always had disagreements about his headgear. To my critical eye, John's hats were disastrous purchases. They suited him so badly that I was sure that he must buy them intentionally to annoy me. They were bizarre and I did not want my husband to look bizarre. On one occasion, in the early days of our marriage, in my absurd detestation of one of his hats, I had taken it from his head and thrown it into the Thames as we were walking along the Embankment. At the time we had both found my impulse funny and John had accepted it as a temperamental but unimportant fit of intolerance. In later years, when the indulgence of early passionate love had passed, I would not have dared to commit such a presumptuous action for it would have released a disproportionately violent reaction. Even as I write the word 'disproportionate' I wonder if it is correct. By removing John's hat and refusing to accept him in it, was I not refusing to accept him as he was but trying to make him conform to what I wanted him to be? I still dislike John's taste in headgear but at least, now, I do accept that it is his taste and his head and does not detract one iota from the way the world regards me. Nobody is going to judge me by the hats my husband wears.

I found it very difficult to learn that we each of us have different attitudes and reactions to every occurrence in our lives. I thought that, because I like being complimented and am prepared to alter something in my dress that is not admired, everybody else must feel the same way. John very rarely either praises or criticises my personal appearance, and accepts me and my choice of clothes without comment; he will go through the motions of admiration if it is demanded of him but I always feel his heart is not in it. He simply does not care. He sees the person, not the trappings, and perhaps he feels rejected when his trappings are despised.

Our first child was born three years after we were married and, having worked up to the week before he was born, I had to learn how to become a full-time housewife. For the first few months, I enjoyed my baby and the experience of being a mother, having time to arrange flowers prettily in the flat, and perform some of the less basic domestic duties for which I had not had time in the past. We had always enjoyed having friends to dinner and being entertained ourselves and, being accustomed to giving little dinner parties as a working wife, I found no difficulty in continuing to do so through the time consuming period of nurturing a small infant. John was now apprenticed and preparing for his intermediate examination, which he passed. Life was fairly happy, perhaps a little dull. I soon found that the coffee-morning set was not for me and did not have the freedom that possession of a car would have given me. From the beginning we had spent our money as it was earned, and John's salary was small. When I stopped earning, we had to be careful. My days tended to be long, as John rarely arrived home before seven, after a drink at the station pub *en route*. When I had a telephone call from my old employer asking if I would care to go back to my job on the same day that I heard of the availability of a trained nursery nurse, I felt that fate had intervened. Believing firmly in common sense rather than any amount of tiresome advice from books on the rearing of babies, I had not heard of John Bowlby and his investigations into maternal deprivation in infancy; but even if I had I think I would have relied heavily on the acknowledgement that an adequate mother-substitute could be as good as a natural mother for the satisfactory emotional development of the child. I engaged the nursery nurse and arranged to return to work full-time after a hand-over period. So, once again, John and I were commuting together in the morning, although I returned alone in the evenings to put my baby to bed. After deduction of my employee's wages, we were still better off than we had been on his salary alone. We were also growing further apart. John was a gregarious man and liked to drink with his friends, and I was more tied down in the evenings than I had been before the arrival of the baby. In a year I was pregnant again and when I left my job this time I knew I would not go back to work so quickly. Towards the end of the period, I also realised that my baby was showing more affection towards his nurse than he was to me and felt that it was necessary for me to spend more time with him. Again I worked right up to the end of my pregnancy. The second baby was not so amenable as the first had been and we had many broken nights. As the days went by I became more and more tired and less and less able to accept with equanimity John's constant habit of arriving home late for dinner, without any telephoned warning. The word 'drinking' became the signal for a flare of temper between us. When he came in, I would kiss him less from affection than as a breathalyser and my first words, after a compressed 'Hallo, darling,' would be 'You've been drinking.' The tenser the atmosphere the more inclined was John to stay away from it; the longer he stayed out the greater the tension to which he returned. There would be evenings when, incensed by my reproaches, he would smash his hand down on the tray I had prepared for him—I no longer waited dinner, knowing that this would only increase my anger and frustration—

and the crockery and food would leap off and crash into a mess of broken china and scattered food on to the floor. Sometimes I would react with fury and shriek at him that he was hateful and selfish, and become an uncontrollable virago, but I soon found that this only released greater anger in him and violence against me. He would stomp out, shouting that I was a rotten wife to come home to, always suspicious, unable to let a man live his own life and relax in the evening; he worked hard all day and his reward was a nag to return to at night. He would slam the front door behind him and leave me, a trembling, whimpering white-faced creature, to clear up the mess and try to gather together the vestiges of my control to enable me to face his later return in silence, knowing that any further reproach would only lead to more bitterness. I would stand at the kitchen window, gazing drearily into the garden, muttering to myself: 'I hate him. I hate him.' When he came back, I would usually be in bed trying to read. I would hear him moving around the kitchen noisily, searching for something to eat, and then, as he banged up the stairs, my stomach muscles would clench with fear that he would begin goading me again. Usually we would not speak to each other and he would undress and get into bed and I would move to the very edge in order not to touch him. Within minutes, his snores would start and I would lie, staring at a triangle of light in the corner of the ceiling thrown up from the street light outside through a gap in the curtains, wondering what had happened to our marriage, trying to understand where I had gone wrong. I could not believe that the kind, easy-going man whom I loved could so quickly turn into the malevolent, unfeeling brute who shouted at me that I was a wicked selfish woman. In the morning, after a bad night, I would wake up drained and he would turn to me and put his arms around me and be kind and loving. I would quietly ask him why he had been so harsh the night before and he would say that he was sorry, that he had behaved appallingly, that he loved me and that he would never behave like that again, and we would hold each other tight in the joy of reunion and another day would make life once again seem full of possibility.

Our days were not always like this. There were weeks when we would be happy together and take great joy in the two little boys who were growing up. Around the time that Michael, our second child, was born in the spring of 1957 we had taken over the house which my parents had rented for years. They were offered it to buy as sitting tenants, but it was a big house and my two sisters were now married and only my younger brother remained at home. The price, even in those days just before the beginning of the sharp upward rise in the cost of property which has continued ever since, was low and John decided that we should buy it. My practical mother saw the advantage of this for everybody. It had been upon her suggestion that, when we were engaged and hopelessly looking for somewhere to live that we could afford, we had taken over and converted the top floor of the house for our home. We had borrowed some money from a relation and had a water supply taken up to the second-floor rooms and had made a kitchen; we had a wash-basin in our bedroom and shared only the bathroom with my parents. With a spare bedroom for James, our first baby, this had been a satisfactory, though not ideal, arrangement. I would have preferred not to have continued to live, after our marriage, in the same house as my parents, but our economic situation had made the arrangement sensible. Because my mother is a woman who knows how not to interfere in other people's lives, we had managed to live almost separately as though it was a fact rather than a formal determined arrangement. Only once do I recall that my mother intervened, and this was when she hesitatingly told me that my relation had informed her that the promised regular repayment of the loan was not being made. This caused the first serious disagreement between John and myself. We had held separate bank accounts when we were both working from which I paid the hire-purchase instalments on our furniture and provided the day-to-day necessities while John was responsible for the bills, the rent and the repayment of the loan. When I broached the subject of repayment to him he brushed me off and I was not happy about his attitude toward his responsibility. For the first time, I searched his pockets one day when I knew he had had a bank statement to find out for myself how recently he had paid anything to my relative. I was sickened to discover that he had not made any payment for several months. He was very angry that I had discovered his default in such an underhand way. The matter was put right but the uneasy feeling I had always had that John's attitude to money was irresponsible was confirmed. He always said that he did not care about money; what I felt he really meant was that he did not care about being solvent and out of debt. He agreed to let me take over the handling of the money and for a while life was smoother, perhaps because he had less to spend and was therefore unable to indulge his drinking habits.

When we took over the house, despite the greater frequency of rows, we were fairly happy. John was completing his apprenticeship, I had accepted my status as a housewife and had more freedom than many young women with small children because, with my parents on the premises to act as baby-sitters, I was able to go out without the complication of having to make special arrangements. The little boys were very fond of their grandparents and to outsiders we appeared a very contented household. John and I exchanged visits with one or two couples in the neighbourhood, had the occasional dinner party, went to the cinema and a rare theatre when we could afford it, and generally gave the impression of living a normal, humdrum suburban life. Only the family doctor and my parents knew of the night that he was called in at midnight by a frightened John to stem the flow of blood pulsing in an unnerving manner from the bridge of my nose after John had hit me violently in the midst of one of our quarrels, and both the doctor and my parents were told by me that I had tripped over and banged my face on the door jamb. My mother could not have failed to hear the shouts and shrieks from the flat above her but she wisely said nothing. The scene occurred a few days before Christmas and I celebrated the occasion that year with two black eyes. How many of my gathered family believed my story I do not know but nobody has ever referred to the occasion since and John was so appalled by the results of his own violence that it was many years before he actually hit me again.

The year after we bought the house, John failed his final examinations, and lost his job. I was desperately disappointed but felt as sorry for him as I did for myself. He had not worked as hard as I would have wished and perhaps he had spent less time than I imagined attending lectures in the last six months of his studies. I had looked forward to the time when he would be qualified and we would have a little more money so that keeping the family would be less of a strain on our limited budget. The evening that John received his result he was so wretched that I telephoned a friend and asked him to come round and help John drown his disappointment in a half-bottle of whisky which I squeezed out of the housekeeping money.

The next day, I telephoned my old employer and asked if he

knew of anybody who wanted a secretary. John and I had agreed that the only thing to do was for me to work for a few months while he stayed at home with the children and revised for the next series of examinations. So once again I became a commuter, and John cared for the boys and worked at his books. For me, those months were happy. James and Michael were as well loved and nurtured by their father as they had been by me; John did not appear to mind doing the domestic tasks, had little opportunity to carouse with his friends, and life was tranquil. As I walked across Green Park to catch my train on those summer evenings, I looked forward to getting home to my family but I enjoyed the contact with people whose lives were not confined to domesticity. I was twenty-eight and full of hope.

On the day that John received notice of another failure, I went up to London in dark glasses. I had wept so much from the disappointment that I could not face the curious gaze of my fellow passengers on the train. There was a delightful young man at my office who was very kind to me that day but he was also realistic. He gently suggested that, as a wife, it was up to me to love my husband and not to make him feel a failure. I went home determined not to add to John's sense of inadequacy by reproaching him in any way. It did not matter if his professional aspirations—or were they mine?—were not to be realised. He would have no difficulty in getting a job, and I would accept that his status would have to be lower than I had hoped. We loved each other, of this I had no doubt, we had our family, our home and our friends, and there was no reason why we could not be happy.

And so for a period we were. There were undoubtedly some tensions in our relationship and I was well aware of the greatest disappointment that married life contained for me, a disappointment of which John appeared to be quite oblivious. I had always been emotional and I found great pleasure and release from tension in sensuality. I loved making love. The slow awakening of sexual desire, the exquisite mounting of sensual pleasure culminating in the ecstasy of fusion was a joy which never failed to turn me into a purring, contented female animal. But as the years of our marriage went by, John lost interest in making love and I lost my femininity and became hard and practical. Sometimes I would bathe and powder and perfume my body before getting into bed, and think: 'Tonight. He must want me tonight'; only to find him, his back to me, reading. I would take my book and read a little too and then he would switch off the light, turn round, put his arm around me and, against the length of my tense, expectant, scented frame, go to sleep. When I tried to caress him into desire, he would say that he was too tired. I found sex and my need for it dominating my thoughts. Waiting to be served at the butcher, I would gaze at the bits of carcase displayed and find that I was not thinking at all about whether or not I could afford stewing steak this week but of the desire that gripped my loins. Sometimes I became so tense with longing that I had consciously to will my mind to mental activity. My discovery of the great satisfaction of intellectual labour was brought about by the self-awareness of my need to manage, somehow, without sexual satisfaction. I had not heard, then, of sublimation but I knew what it was.

Chapter Two

IN THE years that followed, our eldest son started at a local preparatory school. We were not happy for him to attend the primary school, which was in poor accommodation and had a low reputation, and John was now earning enough to make private education just possible if we were careful. We still had no car. Michael attended a morning nursery school, and another baby was on the way. Because of our rare matings, I had long since forgotten about contraception. If John felt the urge, I was not going to risk his losing it and going to sleep while I made the necessary preparations. The pill had not then come into common use.

After eight years, I had abandoned all my early expectations, acknowledging that my marriage was never going to be ecstatically happy but was probably no worse, no better than a lot of others. In finally accepting this, I was helped by having a friend from teenage days who came back to the locality to live. She, also, had an unsuccessful marriage and she was the only person I confided in. I did not lay a great deal of stress on John's drinking, and we both shared financial worries in our lives with our husbands which we blamed for most of our unhappiness. We were wrong, of course, for in each case the acute anxieties that we suffered about our ability to meet last month's bills were but a symptom of much deeper, more subtle causes of stress in our marital relations. Joan and I would have mutual moaning sessions which cheered us up enormously and then, refreshed each by the other's problems, find much in life to enjoy.

David, our third son, was born in the early summer of our ninth year of marriage, and spent his infancy with the sound of typewriter keys clicking through his dreams. The year before, I had started doing copy-typing at home to help boost our income and I worked in a small dressing-room which led off his bedroom. Two and a half years later in 1963 our last son, Andrew, was born. I had by then stopped even trying to cherish my husband since I found that he did not appreciate any thoughtfulness on his behalf, and I turned to my children for comfort and satisfaction. At least they appreciated it if I cooked them a favourite dish or worked late to make them special outfits. I had tried and tried to please my husband. Frequently I had resolved to make myself more careful about my personal appearance so that I should be attractive for him to come home to in the evenings. After the initial disinclination of the morning to get up and face another uncertain day and the helplessness caused by John's refusal to discuss any problems which made the effort to go on so exhausting, once downstairs I would find my spirits lifted by the sun shining in through the kitchen window and the sight of the blossom coming into flower on the apple tree, and it became weak-willed and craven to be daunted by life and stupid to fear the future. I would think that the worsening relationship with my husband must at least in part be my fault and I would resolve to try to recreate a little happiness. I would no longer wander around in my dressing-gown until after breakfast, which I always found demoralising, but would dress and make up so that John had a crisp, fresh wife to greet him when he came down. The children would prefer it too; it was not good for them to become accustomed to a mother whose image was a little sluttish. And so, for a few days, I would persevere. I looked through all my bundles of recipes and found interesting new dishes to cook for the evening meal. One evening, I even climbed up on the kitchen stool and brought down a hidden bottle of sherry from the top of the cupboard and laid it on a tray with two glasses. John and I would drink together. I took extra care with the laying of the table and, after reading James and Michael a bedtime story and tucking them up, rushed into the bedroom to re-do my make-up. I searched for a pair of ear-rings, wishing that I had not lost one of so many of my pairs. I had not worn ear-rings for a long time although, when I was younger, I had regarded myself as incompletely dressed without them, but that was when I had been working and my friends had remarked on my well-groomed appearance. I remembered how the girl who cut my hair had once told me that her husband had seen me in the street one day and had not liked to speak to me, because I looked like a *Vogue* model. I had been gratified by that remark. I had not at all minded being thought aloof, it was a look I cultivated. Now, I did not wish to appear aloof, just attractive.

Feeling chic and serene, I went downstairs and added napkins to the table. We had not used napkins for a long time. The room looked welcoming with fresh flowers on the sideboard by the sherry tray. I went into the kitchen to look in the oven. It was nearly seven o'clock. When John came home I would tell him my plan to join a study class so that I should become more involved with my own interests. I had become far too isolated lately and spent too much time brooding. When I complained to him that I was tired of being domesticated and that he had a far more interesting life than I did, he became impatient with me and told me to make my own life and stop being a drag on him. Perhaps he was right and I should not expect to share his life. I would not complain tonight.

At half-past seven I began listening for his footsteps as he came up the path to the back door. He always came in the back way because he never remembered where he had put his front door key. I went into the dining-room and wondered whether to pour myself a glass of sherry. No, I would wait for John. I wandered to the sitting-room and, lighting a cigarette, picked up the *Radio Times* and leafed through it. Dinner was ready, I had washed the saucepans, remembering to use rubber gloves so that I did not spoil my nails. I had spent some time on my nails and put on varnish. One of the children called, and I took him a glass of water, talked to him for a while, and tucked him up. I came downstairs again and went back into the kitchen. The chops, under their cover in the oven, were beginning to look a little dried up. I walked back into the dining-room and poured myself a glass of sherry after all.

'Damn,' I said. 'Damn.'

I took my glass with me into the sitting-room and turned on the radio. John could have telephoned; he had sworn he would not be late home. I half heard the measured voices discussing some political issue but was too irritable to attend with any interest. Why was John late? Why hadn't he telephoned? I went back to the kitchen and opened the back door to see if he was coming, and then to the dining-room and poured myself another glass of sherry. There was only enough for one more glass in the decanter. I walked round the table and peered out into the garden, my ears straining for the sound of footsteps, then drank my sherry in two gulps and went outside again and down the path to look up the road. There was no sign of him. Back in the kitchen, I took the food out of the oven and helped myself. I sat down at the kitchen table and gloomily ate. 'Blast him,' I thought. 'Perhaps the trains have been held up. I won't mind. He didn't know that I was going to make a special effort this evening.' I picked at some cheese and walked fretfully around eating a banana. Then I took one set of knives and forks off the dining-table and rearranged it for one before going into the sitting-room to read.

When he came in at half-past nine he did not apologise.

'You're late,' I said, trying to make my voice light and un-accusing.

'Yes, I'm sorry. I got held up in the office.'

'Oh. You might have phoned. You said you'd be home by seven.'

'I tried to phone but it was engaged.'

'I haven't been on the phone all evening.'

'Well, it was engaged. There must be something wrong with the phone.'

I felt my anger rise.

'You've been drinking.'

'I just had one on the station while I was waiting for the train.'

'I had planned a good supper, and now it's all spoiled.'

His face, which had worn an open, innocent expression though his eyes did not quite meet mine, darkened in a familiar way.

'You've had yours, haven't you. What's the matter with you? I come home hungry, after a hard day, and you begin carping the moment I come in. All I want is a bit of peace and quiet.'

'Why can't you come home earlier?'

'I told you. I was held up.'

'You always say that. Why don't you phone?'

'I did phone.'

'I don't believe you. You never even think of me. You get together with your friends in the pub and you couldn't care less.'

'Oh, for God's sake, shut up. Where's my dinner?'

'Your dinner's in the oven and you can bloody well get it yourself.'

'You get my dinner and bring it in here.'

'No.'

'Damn you, woman.' He stepped towards me. 'You damn well get my dinner.'

'No.'

He caught hold of my arm and gripped it tightly.

'If you don't get my dinner, I'll bloody well make you.'

'Let go of my arm.'

'Are you going to get my dinner?'

'No.'

He shoved me towards the door and pulled me along the passage to the kitchen.

'Where is it?'

'In the oven, of course.'

'Get it out.'

'No.'

He pushed me hard and I fell against the table, knocking over a stool. He crashed his fist down on the table.

'You will get my dinner out of the oven,' he shouted, banging his fist down on the table at each word.

'Be quiet. You'll wake the children,' I said through tight lips.

'I'll damn well wake anybody I want to. Will you get my dinner out of the oven or not?'

I moved towards the oven, holding my side where it had hit the table.

'All right. But it's only because I don't want you to wake the children,' I said. I picked up an oven cloth and opened the oven door. 'It was a jolly good dinner and now you've ruined it.'

I put the dish down on the table.

'You stupid bitch,' he shouted. 'Why don't you behave like a reasonable wife?'

'Why don't you behave like a reasonable husband?'

'I told you, woman. Now get out of here.'

'No. I want to do some things.'

'Get out.' His face was deeply suffused. 'Or do I have to throw you out?'

I picked up the plate and moved towards the sitting-room.

'Put down that plate.'

'I was only taking it into the other room for you.' I put it back on the table.

'You'll do what I say.' He smashed his fist down on the table again and the plate jerked up and sideways to the floor. The carefully prepared pork chop, its coating of herb-flavoured crumbs withered from its long incarceration, slithered under the table; the buttered french beans spattered the skirting-board.

'Look what you've done. I hate you, I hate you,' I screamed.

'Oh, go to hell.'

He banged out of the kitchen and went down the passage to the sitting-room, crashing the door behind him.

I picked up the chop and put it on a clean plate and into the larder. On these occasions, I always seemed to divide into two separate selves, one involved, angry, infuriated by John's ability to dominate me by force, resistant to the force but concerned not to disturb the children; the other disciplined, knowing just how far the involved self could go and maintaining a watchful control that my own violence did not exceed the limits of my thrifty orderly nature. I would never throw crockery because that would have to be replaced but, on occasion, I would throw hateful, hurtful truths with piercing accuracy, choosing John's most vulnerable spots, not realising and not caring that the patching and repairing of lost respect was far more costly.

As I gathered the scattered vegetables and put them into the wastebin, I felt the hopeless weariness creep over me again. What was the use of trying when John refused to admit that he was ever in the wrong? I could not be at fault all the time. I felt my mouth tight and my jaws aching from the habitual clenching of my teeth. I picked up my packet of cigarettes. Oh God, there were only two left. If I could not sleep and had to get up in the night again to spend it prowling around in an effort to tire myself, I would need more. I took the dog lead from its hook and hunched myself into an old coat hanging in the hall. 'Oh, shut up,' I said angrily to the animal as he scuttered around my legs in excited anticipation of a walk. I went out of the back door and walked drearily down the road; at least the dog benefited from my neurotic dependence on cigarettes. John would not bother to take him out tonight and I would not have walked him more than a few hundred yards if I had not wanted a packet. The cigarette machine was inside the railway station and I knew that I must be a familiar sight to the ticket collector. Old Charley had long since retired. He probably thinks I'm a lonely spinster, I thought. I always come down here by myself and I usually look miserable. I expect he thinks I am dependent on my dog and devoted to him instead of regarding him as a nuisance who drives me crazy with his barking. Feeling guilty at my impatience with the poor beast, I called him to me and bent down to stroke him. His tail wagged as he responded to my touch.

'Come on, Sandy,' I said, and retraced my steps back home, my fingers curling over the comforting feel of the cardboard pack in my pocket. They're my sex substitute, I thought. John never makes love to me any more except when he's very drunk and then he's revolting. I'm getting older and thinner every day and I'm tired. And John is getting coarse and gross.

I let myself in the back way and went up to the bedroom. As I undressed I watched myself in the mirror. 'What's the use of bothering,' I muttered, as I threw my carefully selected clothes on to a chair. 'He doesn't care. He doesn't even see me any more. To hell with him.' I went into the bathroom and smoothed cream over my face, removing my make-up mechanically. I cleaned my teeth and went back to the bedroom. As I took off my bra and pants, again I saw myself in the mirror. My breasts sagged and my legs thinned too much at the thighs so that there was an elongated gap between them upwards from my knees, but I admired my flat stomach and slender waist, and I knew my buttocks looked good in trousers. I wondered if anybody but myself would ever again find pleasure in my body. I put on my nightdress and slid my legs down into the bed, taking care not to pull out the sheet. I lit a cigarette, picked up a book and lay in lonely, accustomed resignation, calm now, one hand propping my head, the other holding the cigarette which my stomach and mouth told me that I did not want but which the habitual nightly ritual compelled me to light automatically. I dozed over my book, waiting for John to come to bed. Cigarette stubbed out, I turned on to my back and lay against the pillows, my eyelids closing and the book fallen on the bedcover. I could hear the radio droning from the sitting-room and guessed that John was stretched out in an armchair, snoringly recumbent.

The next morning I gave the boys breakfast wearing my old dressing-gown with the frayed cuffs. I felt heavy and dull, and it was an effort to move around. I helped Michael to search for his cap, grumbling that he ought to take care of his clothes and not expect me to nanny him. As far as I was concerned he could go to school without it and if he got a detention that was his own fault. His chin quivered and tears began to gather in his eyes. Shamed into being less harsh, I put my arms round him and together we tried to remember the sequence of his actions when he came home the day before. We found the cap in the spare bedroom.

When John came down, the boys had left for school, David was playing in the garden and Andrew was in his pram. John had a grim expression on his face.

'I've decided to clear off,' he said. 'I can't stand this constant questioning and nagging.' He had a small grip in his hand.

'Oh, John,' I said. 'Please don't go. What shall I say to the boys?'

'You can say what you like. I don't know when I'll be back.'

'Please, John,' I begged, and felt my eyes fill with tears.

'Oh, God,' he said. 'Don't cry. You're always crying. I can't stand it.'

I went up to him and tried to put my arms around him.

'I'm sorry I was angry last night,' I said. 'I had made up my mind not to be, but I couldn't help it. I'll try not to do it again. Please don't go.' I clutched at him, trying to draw him to me.

'Get away from me,' he said. 'I'm going.'

'But you can't go, John,' I wept. 'What about Anne's party? We're supposed to be going to her party tonight and I was looking forward to it.'

'Damn Anne's party. You can go to Anne's party. I shan't be here.'

'Please, darling. Please let's try again. I promise I won't get at you any more. Please stay.'

'To hell with you. I'm sick to death. I'm getting out. And for God's sake stop crying. You're always crying.'

'Oh, John. Please don't be so cruel. I can't help crying. You make me cry. I love you so much and I wait for you night after night and when you do come home you're always angry. I can't go on like this.'

'Love,' he said bitterly. 'You don't know what love is. You just want to own me, to live in my pocket.'

'No, I don't. I want to love you, but I'm always by myself and I'm tired of being by myself. I thought when people were married they told each other things. But you never tell me anything.'

'I bloody well work hard all day and when I come home it's to a complaining wife who spends half her time blubbing. I'm bloody well getting out before it drives me mad. Goodbye.'

'Oh, John,' I followed him along the passage to the front door. 'I'm sorry. I'll try to be good, I promise.'

He opened the door and went out without answering. The door

slammed and I mechanically fingered the cracked piece of glass which must surely fall out soon. It couldn't much longer withstand the violent banging the door took every time John walked out in a temper.

I went dully to the telephone in the dining-room and dialled Anne's number.

'Hello, Anne. It's Mary here. Anne, I'm terribly sorry but we shan't be able to come tonight. John has woken up with the most awful cold. He had a sore throat last night but I hoped it would turn out to be nothing so I didn't telephone, but I'm afraid he's feeling rotten now. I am sorry; I was looking forward to it. We both were. No, I'm all right thank you. No, I haven't got a cold, perhaps there's something wrong with the line. I hope you have a nice evening. Yes, I'll tell him. He's sorry too. Goodbye.'

John came home that evening. He said he was sorry and that he would come home earlier in future. He had too much work and it was putting him under strain, but he realised that it wasn't fair on me to let it affect our lives. I accepted his apology but I no longer believed it. It had been made too often before.

And so I stopped trying to cherish my husband.

We still went out together sometimes. Other times, I would go alone. I grew accustomed to making excuses for John's absence. When my hosts expressed regret, I would smile politely and agree with them that it was a great shame he could not be with us. Poor John, he did work too hard, didn't he. When I got home I would usually find him snoring in bed. I would take my nightdress into the bathroom, fumbling under the pillow for it in the dark so as not to disturb him. When he came home after I was in bed, he would walk upstairs to the bedroom with heavy tread, throw open the door and snap on the light and I would pull the covers over my head and pretend to be asleep. This annoyed me so much that I never retaliated by behaving so thoughtlessly myself. When he had thrown off his clothes, often only down to his vest and pants, he would get into bed without bothering to wash and my whole body would tense. I would grip the bedclothes over my shoulder in an effort to prevent my flesh being exposed to the cold air, for he did not slide into bed carefully as I did but would throw the blankets open diagonally as if I weren't there at all. His body would be fleshy and warm and his arm would thrust itself through the gap between my head and shoulder to pull me round and gather me against him to sleep in an embrace. But I would remain taut, my muscles tight against his encroaching body. 'Bloody cold bitch,' he would mutter, and go to sleep, the heavy snoring beginning almost immediately. I would lie, wakeful now, hating him for his grossness, loving him for what he had been. I wondered if I would mind if he died. Sometimes I hated him so much that I wished he was dead and the rest of us could live a happy, normal life, without fear.

When we went out together, I was lively with our friends, and John showed none of the ill-humour that he displayed at home. It was only when we left the company of others that it again asserted itself, and he no longer treated me affectionately.

My ability to wear two faces at the same time confounded John. There were times when I was wondering whether to throw his supper down the lavatory because, once again, it was ruined, that the telephone would ring, and he would say in a friendly voice: 'Darling, I'm sorry I'm late. I've been with Peter and we haven't had any supper. Do you mind if I bring him home?'

'Yes,' I would say.

'Oh, come on, darling. We can't let poor Peter starve. We'll be home in about half an hour.'

Fuming, I would swiftly lay the table and look in the larder to see what I could produce. When they arrived, I would greet the friend with affability and play the charming hostess, but if John followed me out to the kitchen I would turn upon him with venom. These occasions usually ended in equanimity. John had been constrained by his friend's presence from reacting to my recriminations with his usual violence and I, through the success of my act and the calming effect of once again proving to myself how ingenious I was at producing an attractive meal at short notice, and stimulated by the conversation of a third person, had lost my resentment. We would retire together in friendly mood.

John's ability to make me laugh was one of his strongest weapons in undermining my determination not to forgive him. He has a spontaneous, slightly bawdy sense of humour and a verbal wit, when he is not dulled by alcohol, which I envy. He is therefore able to assume the protective mantle of a clown. While my protection from him, after evenings of vituperation and hurtful accusation, was a mask of coldness, he could penetrate it when he chose with a childlike refusal to be serious. He was like the fool of mediaeval days, who turned away his master's ill-humour with nonsense. His contagious laugh was very difficult to resist. This capacity to reduce tragedy to farce, to introduce into pathos a sense of bathos, made him popular among other people. With his good humour in company, and my sense of social fitness which prevented me from showing myself, in public, as the nagging, vindictive wife, we usually succeeded in conveying an impression of marital congeniality which I do not believe any of our friends perceived to be false. I still love his laugh and his maddening ability to undermine my serious intensity of feeling, though I am also irritated by it. And yet, notwithstanding his refusal to take the world too seriously, John always fought life and fate whereas I, despite a tendency to introspection and melancholy, believed that it should be lived and enjoyed and that defeat can always be taken and manipulated into hope. One evening we listened to a recording on the radio of Dylan Thomas speaking his own poetry.

Do not go gentle into that good night.
Rage, rage against the dying of the light.

As that moving voice reached the end of the poem that Thomas wrote on the death of his father, I realised that John was weeping—he was not completely sober. He seemed to have an affinity with the poet, another confused, unhappy human being, fighting to the end against destiny, unable to find a reason for the suffering and cruelty of the world, sensitive to every nuance or inflexion in a look or a word, inferring criticism of himself and lashing out in his pain. One of my favourite pieces of great writing is totally different and I feel suffused with tranquillity whenever I hear it or repeat it to myself.

> Lord, now lettest thou thy servant depart in peace: according to thy word.

I do not fear death, though I do not long for it, and yet there was to come a time when I felt that John, who hated inevitability and had to drink in order to escape from it, might seek it. Despite the peace of the words of the *Nunc Dimittis* in which I found such solace, I did not regard myself as a religious person, was determinedly agnostic against my family background, and stated categorically that I did not consider myself to be a Christian; if death was the end, I was happy to accept it. My concern was to live and not to worry about the impenetrable future. If I could not live my marriage as I had hoped, then I must turn to other things that would be rewarding in themselves, enjoy the days and weeks when John's behaviour was reasonably normal and dismiss from my mind the occasions when he appeared to be in the grip of some alien, demoniacal force.

There came a time, however, when my innate optimism deserted me, when I lay down at night and only wished to find oblivion, not caring whether I woke to another day or not for when I woke I knew that it would be at dawn, with fear clenching me round the guts. As John's drinking became heavier, he forced his guilt upon me. I did not appreciate then the psychological necessity which caused him to reduce me in order that the sense of his own wickedness should be more bearable, the mechanism of defence that converted to attack to project the guilt. I was all the terrible things he accused me of being, a bitch, a nag, an inadequate wife and a rotten mother. When, occasionally, I tentatively asked him why he no longer made love to me, he told me that I was no longer attractive to him, that he required a warm, plump wife. Looking at my drawn face above the protuberance of my collar bones in the mirror, I could understand his distaste. I remembered that the last time he had shown any desire for me was when I was pregnant with our last child. I slept badly and tortured myself with the thought that I did not love the children enough. Certainly the slightest friction between them would evoke violent reactions from me. James suffered most from my outbursts of anger; being less secure, less confident than Michael, he would aggravate a tense situation by argument. For all of us, fearful of the mood their father might be in when he came home, the evenings after school became tight with unexpressed foreboding. Michael would seek to mitigate the tension through withdrawal to his own interests or to appease me by helping with the tea things or entertaining the two smaller boys. James would exacerbate the situation by finding excuse to argue and, being an intelligent, articulate child, he could reason with infuriating logic which sometimes drove me to the extreme of hitting him, my only means of enforcing my will upon him. He would then retire to his room, muttering hate. I always apologised to him and never allowed him to go to sleep without trying to reassure him, but I did not help him to achieve any feeling of stability, and for a long time he suffered at school through his lack of confidence. He so wanted to be loved that he became isolated from other children through his desperate attempts to make himself popular. He hated games, too, which did not help him in his search for acceptance.

Both James and Michael retired early and I rarely had to coax them to bed. They had found that if John came back in a cheerful friendly mood, whilst they were doing their homework, he was determined to assist them and they soon discovered that his help was distracting. Tired from his day, his mind obtuse from alcohol, he would be confused in his explanations and frequently blatantly wrong. Within half an hour, his mood would have changed and they would become involved in the acrimony that seeped into his exchanges with me. The benevolent mood induced by the last drink of the day on his way home would leave him and he became critical and exhausted.

One Friday evening, I came home from a parents' meeting with masters at the boys' school, enthusiastic to tell John how well our sons appeared to be doing, to find him on the telephone. I went out and cleared the supper plates he had left on the kitchen table and took them to the scullery. When I had washed up, he was still talking. I went into the dining-room and he took no notice of me; he appeared to be speaking with some intimacy to the person on the other end of the line. Curiosity aroused, I went to the telephone in the hall and gently lifted the receiver. There was a woman's voice replying to his somewhat inane remarks. I heard him say: 'Keep the bed warm for me tomorrow night.' My reaction was instantaneous and unplanned. I burst into the dining-room, marched across to his unsuspecting back and seized him by the hair as though I would scalp him, shrieking: 'You rotten swine.' He was unprepared as I grabbed the telephone from him and said down it: 'Hello. It's me, Mary, here. I heard what John said to you.' There were gasps at the other end of the line and then protestations of innocence. The woman, whom I knew slightly, said that she was completely flabbergasted by John's suggestion, that she had been trying to fob him off and that certainly there was nothing between them and never had been. We talked together of the unspeakable beastliness of men; I assured her that I believed every word she said, and put down the receiver. As I turned once more to John who had, oddly, stood by whilst I was on the telephone, he suddenly came at me with a look of absolute uncontrollable hatred on his face. I shielded myself as his fist slammed out and then rushed at him again and hammered on his chest in frenzy. He seized my arms and threatened to knock me out and I cowered under his superior strength. He told me tersely to go upstairs to bed. I went. I knew I was beaten. I crawled into the spare bed and lay trembling. I was frightened that he would come and drag me out again, but there was only silence. After a time, I crept out to find my book and clean my teeth. I returned to the spare room and tried to concentrate on reading. An hour or so later I heard his heavy tread on the stairs, and his noisy preparations for bed. Then the bedroom door slammed. I allowed half an hour to pass before I dared to creep downstairs to look for my cigarettes and make a warm drink. As I cautiously trod the stairs back to my room—I knew from practice which of the treads creaked and missed these out keeping to the edge of the whole staircase where the stairs would not sag under my weight —I could hear his snores through the closed door. I hated this man who made my life so miserable and was so unaware that he could sleep immediately he got into bed.

The next morning, he did not try to cajole me into forgiveness. It was Saturday, but James and Michael had to attend morning school, and they had long gone when their father got up. David was playing with his friend along the road, and Andrew was in the flat talking to his grandmother. When John told me that he was packing his bags and leaving, I did not argue. For the first time, I was glad. I didn't want him to stay. I hoped that this time he would not come back. He went upstairs to pack his bag and came into the kitchen to say goodbye. This was unusual. He normally banged out of the house.

'Goodbye,' I said dully.

He hesitated for a moment and then went to the front door. I went heedlessly to the dining-room to watch him walk down the path, but as I opened the door I was petrified by a flutter. A pigeon had fallen down the chimney. I have always been frightened of birds and unable to stay in a room where one is trapped to try to release it. I slammed the door shut and rushed after John. He had turned the corner of the road and was out of sight. I ran to the corner and called to him. He turned round and slowly came back towards me.

'There's a bird in the dining-room. Will you come back and let it out before you go?' I gasped. We walked back to the house together and, putting his bag down in the hall, he went into the dining-room closing the door behind him. I waited outside listening. After a few minutes he came out.

'It's gone now,' he said.

'Thank you.'

He picked up his bag.

'Goodbye,' I said.

He gave me a bleak smile.

'Goodbye.'

And he went.

I returned to the dining-room to see whether the bird had done any damage. The hearth and carpet around it were thick with soot and there were marks on the window and the walls where the bird had defecated in its fear. I fetched a cloth and damped it under the tap, and pulled the vacuum cleaner out from the cupboard under the stairs. As the vacuum drew up the soot I heard myself whimpering. The machine still droning, the pipe still in my hand, I sat down in a chair and laid my head on its arm. I was empty and exhausted and I did not care any more. I did not care about the soot; I did not care about John; I did not care about what I was going to give the boys for lunch. It no longer mattered. Nothing at all mattered. And then, suddenly, a word came into my head. Out of nowhere, the word came and it was important. I said it out loud and it was a revelation. It was hope, it was a chance of help.

'Alcoholic,' I said aloud. 'He's an alcoholic.'

I switched off the cleaner and searched through the A to D telephone book. Did they have an entry or were they ex-directory? It was there. Alcoholics Anonymous. Thank God, I thought. Thank God. I dialled the number and the ring was answered immediately.

'I think my husband is an alcoholic and wonder if you can help me,' I said.

'How did you hear about us?'

'Everybody's heard of *Lost Weekend*,' I said. 'I didn't see it but I know about it.'

'Why do you think your husband is an alcoholic?'

I told him about John's behaviour.

'It certainly sounds as though he may be. Does he drink first thing in the morning?'

'I don't know. He certainly starts at midday.'

'I'm afraid we can't do anything unless he asks for help himself.'

'He won't do that,' I said. 'He doesn't think there's anything wrong with him. He tells me that I'm neurotic and blames it all on me.'

'That's normal. I'm sorry for you, but we can only help when *he* wants help.'

I wept again then. I wept into the telephone and released all the suppressed anxieties and worries to the first sympathetic ear that I had sought. He was kind and understanding and he told me that his name was Bob and that if ever I wanted to talk to him again I only had to call that number and he would be available.

I was sad when I put down the receiver, but I felt a little better. I had been confirmed in my sudden inspiration and now I knew that there was somebody to turn to for comfort.

With a lighter mood upon me, tension released and the beginning of comprehension, I returned to clearing up the soot. After I had finished, I thought to go and find David, and went up to the bathroom to wash and make up my face. I held a cold flannel to my swollen eyes, and took care with my make-up. I walked up the road. David was playing in the garden of his friend's house and I saw his mother through the kitchen window. I rang the doorbell and she warmly invited me in. Warmth was a word that I always associated with Diana. We had known her and her husband Bill for some years and, although not close friends, we had entertained each other spasmodically. When I acted as hostess, she always gave me the feeling that I performed the role superbly, that only I could manage to rear four sons and produce a delicious meal with such imperturbable ease. She built me up in my own estimation and there was no undercurrent of criticism in anything she said. She had something I envied, the ability to accept other people as they were and make them appear better. She was enthusiastic without being boring in her enthusiasm, optimistic without being unrealistic. Her reaction in any setback or disaster was not resentment or dismay that it had happened to her, but an apparently easy acceptance which enabled her to find a way of living through it with the certainty that it would pass, that February always does lead to June. Her favourite expression when faced with the anger or resentment of others was, 'Oh, life's too short,' implying a refusal to be associated with such negative attitudes. But her feeling for those in trouble was not dismissive, it was only her own problems that she seemed to dismiss with such ease. To the problems of others, she gave thoughtful attention and communicated her belief in the ephemerality of the moment; she gave love and attention and unstinting time. In the months to come I found that I could rely on Diana. She never made me feel that I was a nuisance, that my problems were none of her business and, although she could not solve them, she could and did build me up and enable me to return to my unhappy home stabilised by the intuitive understanding of the response I needed, whether it be unreserved affection or a square meal or, on some occasions, a bed to sleep in undisturbed.

That day, without knowing of her deep compassion that I had yet to experience, but conscious of her unreserved friendliness, I sat on the kitchen table and began to chat. And then, once again, the tears started.

'John's walked out on me,' I said. 'We had a terrible row last night and he's gone.'

'Come and have lunch with us,' she said.

Her husband came into the room.

'Hello, Mary,' he said, ignoring my splotched face.

'Mary and the boys are having lunch with us,' said Diana.

'Good,' said her husband.

'Bill,' I said. 'Do you think John's an alcoholic?'

He was a reserved man who, in the company of others, preferred conversation to be kept at a conventional level and refused to be drawn into heated discussion. He laughed affectionately at his wife's excesses of enthusiasm and I was never sure of how he felt about anything. I cannot imagine him being angry, or ecstatic, or anything but the stolid, reliable Bill I liked but felt I would never really know. My question was unfair, taking him by surprise and demanding instant and very personal evaluation of somebody who, being a man with whom he was on friendly terms, he would naturally feel he must not betray.

'I don't know,' he said guardedly. 'Do you think he is?'

'Yes,' I said.

'Never mind,' said Diana. 'Come and have lunch and everything will look a little brighter.'

I went home to make the beds and fetch Andrew and returned to my friends for lunch. I was surprised to find that I was very hungry. Diana let me help her with the dishes and we sat down with coffee.

'You know, Mary,' Diana said, when I left, 'we are always here. Come any time you feel you need to.'

I was grateful for the promise of sanctuary.

As I turned down our front path, I heard the sound of the lawn-mower. John was mowing the back lawn.

For the rest of the day, we were polite to each other, the boys seemed unaware of the underlying tension and John stayed at home and played with them after the sun had gone down, and when he went out really did only take the dog for a walk.

The next morning, after a night spent alongside but together in our matrimonial bed, John put his arms around me and said that he was sorry for what had happened.

'It was a terrible thing to do,' he said. 'It will never happen again.'

Drowsy, enfolded by his warmth and lulled by his obvious compunction, I nevertheless had to ask him.

'Are you having an affair with that woman?'

'Of course I'm not,' he said fervently. 'I can't think why I made such a stupid suggestion. I did have rather a lot to drink on Friday but I shouldn't have behaved like that. But I won't any more. I shall become a reformed character.'

I wanted to believe his words but I had heard them before too often. I let them pass.

'Darling,' he said, as he kissed my eyes. 'You know you're the only woman I've ever loved, don't you.'

'Yes,' I said. I did believe that. John had never shown any interest in women and I had always felt completely secure in this one aspect and trusted him. I knew he lied to me, about money, about his late homecomings, about drinking, but not about this, even though he did not often demonstrate his love. I had never questioned, even in my own mind, his fidelity.

We all enjoyed that day. In our reunion, we were happy. For once John did not go down to the station, ostensibly for the Sunday papers. So often, Sunday lunch was a terse occasion, delayed because of John's late return from the pub. He would try to be jovial but I would be tight-lipped in my annoyance that we had all been kept waiting, loathe to express my anger as it would upset the boys. By the time the meal was over, the alcohol in John and my coldness to him had turned him sour and, although he helped with the washing-up, it was with a tetchiness that made the boys clear the table in silence, anxious not to do anything to enrage him. In the afternoon he would sit in a deck-chair in the garden or in an armchair in front of the fire and fall asleep, his mouth falling slack, the heavy pouches under his eyes accentuated by the relaxation of his muscles. I disliked Sunday evenings, when he would become taciturn and I began to anticipate another week of his absence in the day and the deterioration of his mood from Monday, when he usually returned home at a reasonable hour, to Friday when he would have reverted to the practice of not turning up until nearly bedtime. But this Sunday, we were together with the children all day and I once again experienced the rare pleasure of a united family.

Chapter Three

FROM THAT that week-end, I began to recover something of my own identity. Attaching a word to John's confusing, irrational behaviour seemed to make it more bearable. If he was an alcoholic, and there were times when life was comparatively peaceful that I doubted it, then it was not me and my attitude which caused the terrifying outbursts. I was not neurotic—not congenitally so. My neurosis, if it existed, was an understandable reaction to his abrupt changes of mood, his complete unreliability. I no longer believed him when he told me that I had no idea what life was about, that I had no conception of the pressure of a working life. When he sneered and suggested that I would like a timid, obedient husband, rigidly clocking in at 9 a.m. and out at 5 p.m., I no longer saw, through his eyes, the boredom of a conventional suburban life, spontaneity dulled by routine and platitude, but imagined the joy of sharing in the interested development of our children, the pleasure of fulfilling joint plans which were not forgotten the day after they were made. I knew, however, that I must cast aside all such yearnings, that John was not going to undergo a metamorphosis and become, suddenly, an honest, dependable husband. He accused me sometimes of provoking rows for their own sake, saying that I could not live without tension. Though he was wrong in seeking to transfer the responsibility of provocation to me, there was some truth in what he said about the tension. For I was bored, not by familiarity, but by loneliness. I talked to nobody of my problems, not even to Diana and Bill after that momentary lapse, for Diana was a full-time working woman with an *au pair* to care for her young son, and there was no opportunity for the intimate exchange of confidences which result from the frequent encounters of neighbouring housebound mothers. Tied to my home as I was by small children, I had little stimulating company. We went out to tea and had other children, with their mothers, to tea with us, but I found domestic conversation dull and lacked contact with people who thought beyond the humdrum events of their immediate environment. I lived each day, going about my tasks mechanically, feeling like a zombie. I tried to take a lively interest in my children's concerns but lacking dynamism myself I found it difficult to convey the vitality of curiosity and intellectual growth to them. When John and I quarrelled, at least I felt alive, my mind came into action as I sought for the most wounding, incisive retaliation to his blundering attacks before I was overcome by physical force, or my own hysteria, and became a weeping, incoherent mass of self-pity.

Shortly after my revelation of understanding, I took a morning job with a consultant psychiatrist at a local hospital. In my new determination to live my own life and detach myself from my disappointing husband, I had decided that I must get out and do something positive. I arranged an *au pair* for six months to look after the little boys, one of whom now attended nursery school. My salary covered the cost of keeping her and, though the financial gain would be negligible, I felt that the psychological benefit to me would make worth while the possible embarrassment of having an outsider resident to witness my husband's attacks of insanity. In the event, the very presence of an observer caused him to restrain himself and, though it must have been apparent that our family life was strained, there was little outright quarrelling in the time that she was with us. My employer was shortly going abroad for a year and wanted a secretary for three months to help him get on to paper some research on which he was working and to attend and précis the seminars which he led among a group of social workers. I found the work interesting and my boss seemed pleased with my ability to abstract the purport of discussion, though I was disappointed to find that I spent most of my working hours in an office by myself. Dr. Martin had at that time a research psychiatrist working under him, a student from abroad. He was a homely, kind young man, anxious to complete his research before he returned to his own country but suffering from an uncertainty about his own ability and from the slight antagonism which he felt towards him, so often subtly conveyed though not openly expressed towards a foreigner by the natives of his host country. He had nobody to type up his research work and, although his English was adequate for day-to-day conversation, his prose style and command of the nuances of the language were not sufficiently developed for the presentation of papers to learned publications. He occasionally came to the office where I worked to talk to Dr. Martin, and I was friendly, for which he appeared grateful. When I learnt of his difficulties, I suggested that when my three months' engagement with Dr. Martin was over, if I could work at home, I should type his manuscripts for him. My *au pair* girl was due to leave me in the spring and I had not arranged another job. Dr. Bergman was pleased to accept my offer. It was a delightful summer: Dr. Bergman came to my house one or two days a week and we sat on deckchairs in the garden while he carefully explained his concepts to me and then left me with his confusion of papers. Flanked by *The Oxford English Dictionary* and Roget's *Thesaurus*, I would sit at my typewriter manipulating his clumsy sentences into readable prose. It was a difficult task for I had to be sure that I first understood what he was trying to convey and not change the essence of his thinking in the writing. Tricky though it was, I enjoyed the new experience of applying my mind to an activity which required an exercise of intellect. Dr. Bergman was demonstrably gratified by the result and almost embarrassingly thankful to me for having helped him. Before he left England, he invited me to take the children to tea at the hospital with him and his wife, and he later sent me an offprint of one of his papers which was published.

That short acquaintance helped me out of all proportion to the impulse that prompted me to offer my services to Dr. Bergman. I had for so long believed John when he derogated my capacity to think clearly that I had lost confidence in any pretensions I might have had to mental ability. Now, after working first for Dr. Martin and then for Dr. Bergman, I knew I was not a fool, that men who were intellectually able regarded me as capable and intelligent. My new knowledge of myself gave me an impregnable armour against John's need to detract from my self-esteem in order to protect himself from the necessity of turning an objective eye upon his own behaviour. When he derided me, I no longer felt that maybe he was right, that I was stupid and had led such a protected life that I had no conception of what real living was like. I knew I had a lot to learn, but I began to trust my own perceptions and to build upon this new self-confidence.

Shortly after the birth of Andrew in 1963, John had sat his final examinations again and passed, five years after his original attempt. After his earlier failures, he had worked in the same profession, unqualified, with several firms, and I had dismissed all thought of his ever qualifying. He was reasonably paid, although with school fees to be met we were always hard up and we still had no car. When he announced his decision to sit the examination again, I was glad but not sanguine. I encouraged him by my non-interference rather than with any positive enthusiasm. He appeared serious in his intent and became less extreme in his behaviour. He was certainly drinking less and this affected our lives advantageously. Although there were still evasions and a disregard for economic security which resulted in frequent financial crises, there also appeared to be a new sense of responsibility. He had never insured himself, so that any accident to John would have reduced us to instant poverty, but I had acquired the ability to ignore any possible chance of disaster in the future and learnt to live in a bearable present. John's taste in clothes was expensive and I deplored his contention that everybody kept their tailors waiting to be paid. On one occasion, it was not until a writ was issued that he finally agreed to pay for a suit. I spent very little upon myself, enjoying making my own clothes and finding a certain pride in stretching a budget that seemed incapable of meeting the demands upon it. This must have been one of the periods when I was allowed to control the finances of the family, and John had nothing but pocket money. I learnt to search for bills in his dressing-gown pocket where they were stuffed on arrival and remained until I found them. With John studying, we entertained very little and on the rare occasions when we bought spirits or wine to offer our guests, I made a habit of hiding them the next day so that we had a reserve for the next time. The day that John's results were announced, he telephoned me excitedly to say that he was through, that at last he was qualified. I was pleased, and yet I felt an underlying sense of foreboding that mitigated my pleasure. On that day, David was attending a birthday party. I was slightly appalled when John walked in at half-past five in the evening, a fat cigar protruding from his flushed face, full of his own success and alcohol, and told me that he had been to fetch David on his way home but that the party had not ended. His inebriation must have been obvious to David's hostess.

A month later, again he telephoned me during the day to tell me that he was throwing in his job and starting on his own. I had no choice but to accept this impetuous decision since he had already told his employer that he was leaving. All his changes of job had been made in this way, without warning, without discussion, a sudden decision to walk out. As he always found himself another job immediately I had no cause to complain, but I did sometimes wonder whether he had really been fired.

This time, though, was different. Finding another job did not appear to be difficult, but I felt that the risk of starting on his own, without capital, was foolhardy. Nevertheless, John appeared confident, said he had many contacts which, knowing his popularity, I did not doubt, and I had enough money to see us through the next month; he also appeared to be on good terms with his bank manager, a new one. Of the big five banks, there was not one to which John had not transferred his account over the years when the previous one refused to allow him credit any longer. His power to persuade was not confined to me, who loved him and longed to be in accord with him; bank managers, too, found his charm and plausibility irresistible. I was still involved with my work for Dr. Bergman, which prevented me from brooding, and life began to take on new possibilities as John's confidence proved to be justified. He bought a car and we both passed the driving test. We had now been married for fourteen years. James, at eleven, was attending a public day school, Michael was still at preparatory school, David was due to join him in the autumn, and Andrew began going to nursery school. Financially, for the first time, living became easier. John's business began to flourish and he needed a secretary. With the termination of Dr. Bergman's work, I agreed to go to his office on one or two mornings a week to help him. I disliked working at the office because John was unpredictable and was often out, but he began bringing work home in the evening for me to type at high speed after supper to rush down to catch the last post from the post office. We managed for a short time in this way, and then I applied to a secretarial agency to get him a full-time secretary. He was lucky. The first girl who came to see him arrived just as I was leaving the office and impressed me with her look of competence and reliability and as I went out of the door I whispered to John: 'Take her.' He did, and she proved herself compatible with her looks.

Once again, I was homebound. Once again, our domestic life

began to deteriorate. One day, I telephoned John at his office to be told he was out. I asked for his secretary—he shared a telephone switchboard with the other firm in the building. She was out too. I thought little of this and was amazed when he came home in the evening, in a mood of uncontrollable anger, to accuse me of snooping on him, trying to discover what he was doing in the day-time. I tried to defend myself in my innocence and an event which I had not registered as important, the fact that he and his secretary were both out at the same time, suddenly became fraught with suspicion. I decided that the only way to maintain my peace of mind was to avoid telephoning him at all.

Having discovered the need and restorative power of leading my own life and found, as a result of my work with Dr. Bergman, that intellectual activity alleviated much of my emotional tension, I enrolled that autumn for a four-year diploma course. This meant attending one morning lecture a week and undertaking at home as much study as I could manage, and I found great satisfaction in meeting people who were mentally active. As John's business increased, there seemed to be a lot more money available, although I still felt that it was not being spent on the right things, but I managed to suppress my uneasiness. I was now given a monthly cheque for household commitments, which included rates, and John was responsible for mortgage repayments and school bills. One morning, the secretary of the boys' preparatory school telephoned. I knew her slightly and she was friendly. She said that she had been instructed by the bursar to telephone the parents who had not paid that term's accounts. I told her that I had no idea that it had not been paid and would certainly do something about it. As John had recently decided that it was time that we laid in a store of wine and had had a rack built into the cellar to accommodate 300 bottles, I had imagined that our finances really were, for the first time in our married life, secure. I greeted him when he came home that evening with angry accusations and the suggestion that he had his priorities wrong. As usual, he accused me of being hopelessly untrusting. If I would only leave him to do things 'in his own way', a frequent expression, and not interfere, life would be much smoother. By some alchemy of reasoning, he appeared satisfied that his broad approach to the economic management of our lives would, in the end, show how wise he was, that it was necessary to take risks and expend our small resources for greater return, and that I just did not understand how business worked. How could he entertain the right sort of client without a wine cellar? I was left to find the money for the school bill.

I realised now that I could no longer allow myself to be deluded into pretending that our financial state was solvent. I knew that he had a large overdraft. Because any mention of money caused friction and explosive anger, and I feared rows not only for myself but for the children, I learnt to restrain myself from mentioning my acute anxiety until John appeared to be in receptive and co-operative mood. I was loathe to risk the possibility of spoiling what might otherwise be a peaceful evening, and waited for the week-end, when there might be time to talk in a less hurried manner than was possible in the few minutes after the boys had gone to school and before John left for his office. He was always more tractable in the mornings. Usually the bills which involved the family were paid in the end; the bills which were his own concern I decided to ignore.

As the weeks of my first year's course proceeded, I immersed myself more and more in my books. If John came home late, I no longer had to restrain my anger because I no longer thought about him. I turned to my studies and forgot him. When he opened a second office, I expressed doubts as to the wisdom of such a venture so soon but was told that it was necessary to expand, that the work was there and that this was the way to grow rich. He had builders in to partition rooms, employed more staff, and suggested that I might like to organise the carpeting for him. Unable to believe that he would be so unwise as to incur all this expenditure unless he was confident of his ability to meet it, once again I rejected caution and did as he asked. After all, his first office did appear to be very busy, despite our monetary squabbles our standard of living was higher than it had ever been, we still had the car and the boys were still at their fee-paying schools. Perhaps I was over-anxious and John's refusal to manage his personal expenditure in a way that met with my approval was simply something that I had to put up with and mitigate as best I could. At least he was now insured.

I became conscious that he resented my increasing independence from him. One evening, as I was struggling with an essay at the kitchen table (I worked in the kitchen which was warm in order to avoid the expense of heating another room for I was always careful not to incur unnecessary bills), he walked in from the sitting-room where he had been watching television and scornfully derided my studiousness. I took no notice, and he went to bed while I continued with my work.

He began saying that he needed my help in the office. His first secretary had left him to have a baby, another was occupied working for an assistant in his first office and he could not get competent girls for his new office. He now employed two assistants there, too. I said that I disliked working for him, that I found the way he worked did not accord with my view of the way an office should be organised and I did not wish to be involved. He appeared to accept this. My first examination was imminent, and my own life was fuller and more satisfying than it had been for years.

It was a strange, separated life that we led, for John rarely remembered to tell me of any arrangement he had made which concerned me. One day, I was entertaining a mother in the garden with her two small children, the little boys all playing together as we talked, when the front door bell rang and I found two men on the doorstep who had come to treat the woodworm in the cellar stairs. I knew that we had woodworm but had no idea that John had arranged for it to be dealt with. I hastily excused myself from my guest and dragged the contents of the cellar clear before the men started spraying, then returned to my friend in the garden, and we spent the rest of the afternoon moving our deckchairs further and further down the lawn as fumes of noxious spray drifted out of the cellar window and enveloped us.

Another day, I opened the door to find two hulking men and a van which they had backed up the path to the front door step.

'Night storage heaters,' one said.

'What do you mean?' I asked. 'We haven't got any night storage heaters.'

'We've come to deliver them.'

'But I haven't ordered any.'

The man looked at the address on the piece of paper he held, and confirmed that he was at the correct house.

'Perhaps your husband knows about them,' he said.

'Just a minute. Come in, and I'll telephone to find out.'

'Oh, yes,' said John, over the telephone. 'I forgot to tell you. I thought they'd be a good idea. I got them second-hand. They were cheap.'

I returned to the men waiting impatiently in the hall and told them to give me time to work out where to put them. They were massive, industrial-type heaters, and I was not inclined to ruin my drawing-room with such ugly equipment. I decided that the hall and the playroom would be the most suitable places and they were built in. They were not attractive, but they did create a pleasant warmth in our large, late Victorian house which we still heated with coal fires.

Although I accepted the storage heaters, I could not long tolerate the brussels sprouts in the front garden. I remembered John planting some seeds but as they grew to recognisable form, I doubted my vision. I asked him why he had decided to grow vegetables in the front garden when we had a perfectly good patch at the back for them.

'Don't be so conventional,' he said. 'Why shouldn't we grow vegetables in the front garden? You always say we ought to grow more of our own produce.'

I left them for a while but managed to extract them without causing uproar before they became too unsightly and began to smell like a smallholding.

One night over dinner, when we were friendly, it must have been on a Monday or a Tuesday, I told John that I was thinking of joining a local choir. I had enjoyed singing in my school choir years ago and I had read a plea for more members.

'I might join, too,' he said.

'Will you really, John,' I said, amazed. 'I'll telephone the conductor right away and ask if he'll have us.'

Choir practice was on a Friday night, and for the first concert we both regularly appeared for rehearsals. The choir was singing Haydn's *Creation* and, working on it, I learned to love it. John bought the record album and we listened to it with our scores in front of us. We were often a little late for choir practice as John invariably only just arrived home in time for us to drive to the hall, but this was a great improvement on our accustomed Friday evenings. Our first concert over, the choir disbanded for the summer to meet again in the autumn. Once again, John came with me, at first. But he dropped out shortly after. I was glad, for he always smelt heavily of whisky and I shuddered for the men who flanked him in the bass section. He also tended to come in at the wrong moment, a note or so early. I did not turn round to identify him, but I knew whose voice it was. Shortly after he decided that he was too busy to come to choir practice—I suspect that it was a great relief to our choir master—I had to leave myself. He would arrive home too late for me to drive myself there, somehow always needing the car himself on Fridays, and the distance was too far for me to walk, so I reluctantly resigned.

Then John decided that, to promote business, he must play golf. He bought himself an expensive set of golf clubs and joined two clubs; they both had high subscriptions. He always delighted in immoderate participation.

When he was proposed and accepted as a member of the RAC Country Club, he told me what a great honour it was to be elected to such an élite association, as though it was the Athenaeum. We went there to dinner one night and I noticed a table containing a mass of pot plants and flowers. When I asked our host what they were for, he told me laughingly that they were for husbands to take home to their wives when they were late for lunch. I was not amused. In the past, John had sometimes come in with a bunch of flowers to placate me and I always regarded such offerings with suspicion. That the Club should pander to such hypocrisy and really believe that it paid off damned it for me.

We shared the car and on the days when it was agreed that I should have it, I would take John to work, before he moved up to London, and fetch him in the evenings if he telephoned for me. One day, just before Christmas, I arrived at his office to find him in an amiable mood. As I was weaving my way through heavy traffic, he produced a ring box from his pocket and told me that, after all these years, he had bought me the engagement ring which I had never had. It was a large solitaire diamond. I was touched that he wished to make up to me for the disappointment in the lack of that romantic token which I had felt so long ago, though at the time my practical mind had not allowed my sentimental heart to care too much. I was confident that our love did not need symbols. Now the diamond, presented in such unsuitable circumstances amidst the turmoil of home-bound traffic, seemed to represent a token not of love, but of our unaccustomed material security, a guarantee that the days of struggling to meet bills and maintain a reasonable standard of living were over. I had never felt that we had enough to spare for luxuries; most of our furniture was second-hand and I made clothes for the boys for as long as it was possible until it became necessary to buy school uniform. I had little pride and recall vividly a day in a local school outfitters when a customer beside me, whose son went to the same school as mine, was buying items of uniform for her child. As she bought a raincoat, I said in a friendly voice, thinking to benefit her: 'Do you know, I've never spent more than ten shillings for a raincoat. They have marvellous ones at the school sales.' She looked at me with disdain. If John could now afford to buy me a diamong ring, the money must be coming in; I knew that I must continue, as far as I could control it, to take care that it was wisely used but felt that the motive behind the purchase of the ring compelled me to accept it graciously and without question. When the ring was followed by a diamond pendant, I knew that this new extravagance must be discouraged. Besides, I had no desire to amass expensive baubles. When I demurred that we really could not afford them, John said that he wanted to have something for us to hand down to our children, that he felt the need for heirlooms. I only wore the pendant once and felt no pleasure in it.

At a time when most people had succumbed to the draw of television, we still did not have one. I disliked the thought of that ubiquitous screen dominating my leisure, and subscribed vehemently to the attitude that it was harmful to the development of children and their ability to entertain themselves. For as long as our resources were obviously strained, John had not pressed his wish for a television set. On the evenings that he was at home, he usually went to bed early, leaving me with my sewing and the radio, or my books. Shortly after he had started his own firm, he came home on Saturday and, taking David with him, said he was going to buy a television set. I was very angry. I had not been consulted. The set was delivered the following week, to the delight of the boys. We had acquired from my parents a heavy mahogany screen which, in the winter, we used as a draught excluder around the sitting-room door. I was so offended by the sight of that blank white square imposing its dominance in the corner of my beautiful drawing-room—the one room in the house which I cherished because of its fine proportions and carefully guarded immunity from the paraphernalia of children's activities—that I shielded my affronted eyes by placing the screen around the television set when it was not in use. When, the following week, a technician arrived to adjust our new set, I took him into the room.

'Where is it?' he said, looking round blankly.

I removed the screen, feeling a little foolish, and I did not put it back again.

I realise now that living with a man subject to irrational, impulsive acts affected my own reasoning badly. I felt a deep urge for order and co-operation in our lives and, because we lacked this, I swung to an extreme of intolerance of spontaneity which was as neurotic as the behaviour which provoked it. Because John did bring home many useless objects which were an embarrassment or an extravagance that we could ill afford, I extended my critical judgement of his taste and wisdom to everything he did. We really did not want the six refrigerator shelves which he picked up as a bargain—we had not even got a refrigerator—but the shade he bought for the porch light to cover the bare bulb which had swung from its flex for so long was pretty, though I would not admit it. The heavy Victorian sideboard which arrived one week-end was an excrescence and a nuisance because it was difficult to clean the dust from its complicated, protuberant decorative trimmings, the doors fell off their hinges every time they were opened, and we did not need it anyway. But it was kind of him to give house-room to some of the more essential or treasured items of furniture of a bankrupt acquaintance before the the bailiffs moved in on her so that the poor old thing was not completely bereft, even though we were unable to use the drawing-room for as long as they remained with us.

I had learnt how to cope with his moods. At night he was intractable and would frequently express the intention of taking the car the next day when I had arranged some outing and it was my turn for it anyway. I soon discovered that if I raised no objection and did not try to instil a sense of fairness about keeping to prior arrangements, invariably when morning came he had decided he did not want it after all. It was not necessary to cancel all my arrangements, only to acquiesce in the evening because he would have forgotten by morning his imperative need for it anyway. Thus I learnt the value of passivity.

We rarely went out together now and on the rare occasions when we did, John's company was less lively than it had been. His contribution to any discussion was uninformed and dull; he could be relied upon to repeat a few moth-eaten jokes and I would sit, politely smiling, wondering how many more times I could listen to them without screaming. At the end of such an evening we would drive home in silence. Fortunately for my peace of mind and safety, he generally allowed me to drive—an unusual concession in an alcoholic—settling himself in the back seat as though I was his chauffeur.

I took my first examination on a Saturday, after two terms' study. On the Monday morning, as I was busying myself around the house, beginning to catch up on all the neglected tasks and planning a domestically productive summer before the second year's course began in September, the telephone rang.

'You must come to the office. I need you,' John said. There was urgency, near desperation, in his voice.

'I'll come tomorrow,' I said.

The next morning, I drove the boys to school, and then followed John to London on a late commuters' train.

Chapter Four

I THOUGHT at first that I must break under the shock and strain. I had known for a long time that I was curtaining off a part of my mind to keep myself from consciously recognising how sick our life was. I had persuaded myself that, if I ignored the things that I did not want to know about, perhaps they would go away. My introduction to John's business life destroyed any illusions I had managed to retain. Within the first week, I discovered the chaos which dominated his life. He employed two assistants, an accountant and two typists. He had also recently taken into partnership an old friend, who ran the original office. One of the assistants had worked in another firm with John in the past, and was fond of him. Amidst the confusion, he tried to work a steady day. The other was a young man. John was out a great deal of the time, never came back when he had promised, but refused to allow anybody but himself to open the post which meant that it frequently remained unopened. When he was out, I went into his room and stole it so that some of the work could be carried on. I opened cupboards and found piles of unanswered correspondence, angry letters seeking explanations for delay, office accounts unpaid. One morning when the young assistant was dictating his letters to me, I asked him why he stayed. He told me that he was fascinated to watch how things developed, although he was sorry for me and the children. He was pleasant enough, but I despised his dispassionate interest. I imagine that he was looking for another job at the time but was holding on, for as long as his salary continued to be paid to him, until he found one and, in the meantime, took a wry interest in the situation. I soon realised that the accountant was not helping my husband. One morning, when I tried to open the door of John's office, I found it locked. I knew that he and the accountant were inside and hammered on the panels, demanding to be let in. I heard a clink of glass, then John unlocked the door. I walked straight to his desk and opened a top drawer: inside were a bottle of whisky and two glasses. I looked at them both and vented my contempt.

I realised that John was completely incapable and that I would have to take over, not only the responsibility of our domestic life which I had carried for so long, but also deal with his business as soon as I could see how. In the meantime, I attempted to introduce some sort of order but it was an impossible Herculean task. Each day I caught a train home in time to fetch the boys from school. As I sat in the compartment, attempting to read a newspaper or a book, the whole appalling weight of impending disaster descended upon me. In order that my intense anxiety should not communicate itself to the boys, I immersed myself immediately we arrived home in violent physical activity, cleaning the car, digging the garden, making inane, inattentive conversation with them. The routine of those few weeks was for John to drive the boys to school, leaving me to wash up the breakfast and make the beds before I followed him to London. We had an agreed place for leaving the car so that I could drive from the station to fetch the children in the afternoon. Sometimes, when I reached our suburb and left the station to get the car, it was not there and I had to run a mile to the school to arrive on time and walk the boys home. One afternoon, as I was panting along the road, tired, sick with fear, angry at this additional unnecessary effort, and emotionally exhausted by my inability to extract from John any admission that there was anything wrong, to make him face the situation he was in, a car stopped and a friend leaned across to offer me a lift. We picked up our children and she drove us home. I explained that I had lost the car, and then burst into tears. She sent the children into the garden to play, and turned to me.

'It's something to do with John's drinking, isn't it?' she asked.

I nodded.

'I always thought there was something wrong,' she said. She was a fairly recent acquaintance whom I had come to know through the boys. 'With John in the position he is, I wondered why your house was so shabby, why you seemed unable to afford so many things. I have had experience of this before—my father had a friend, and the same thing happened to him.'

'I don't know what do do,' I said. 'He won't admit anything.'

She tried to comfort me, but she could not help.

That night, I looked at John when he came in. Over the past

two years, he had put on so much weight that there was no line to his jaw and the flesh of his neck puffed around his ears. His stomach was protuberant and heavy, like that of an old, self-indulgent man and there was a coarseness about him which made him look ten more than his forty years. The only compensation, to my critical eyes, was that he no longer walked with rounded shoulders and I was reminded of a sentence, written by I have forgotten whom, that we had once laughed over: 'His stomach was a monument to the strength of his back.' His eyelids were thick and his eyes protuberant and always slightly glazed, and when he looked at me he never looked direct but always slightly past me as though he was not focusing. I had the sensation that he looked through me at an object behind my head as if I were transparent, with no more substance than a ghost. I found it difficult to see him without revulsion, when I truly looked. He had an enormous stomach. I scarcely bothered to cook for him for he rarely ate the food. He was often sick and told me that this was caused through worry and strain, which he put down to the incompetence of his staff. For a long time, I had chosen to appear to believe him, but now we both of us knew that I could no longer take part in this charade. Suddenly, through all the torment and pain of hopelessness and despair, of frantic attempts to remain steady with the boys and show no sign of my desolation, I had a surge of hope. I remembered how, two years before, an anonymous voice had told me that help was available when the sufferer acknowledged his own desperation. I felt that the time was near when John might admit that he needed help.

The next day, after John had left, I telephoned Alcoholics Anonymous again and asked for Bob. I had kept the name, written on a scrap of paper, in my purse. Another voice told me that AA did not work through individuals but that he was there to help me if he could. He told me about an organisation which existed alongside AA called Al-Anon, for the families of alcoholics. Many had found great strength in sharing their experiences. Al-Anon worked anonymously, too, so that if I wished for someone to be put in touch with me, I should give him my telephone number and first name. I said that I would.

Within an hour, Jill telephoned and identified herself as an Al-Anon member. She listened to my story. I told her how terribly difficult I was finding it to remain calm with my children.

'When I was going through what you are now,' she said, 'my

son was very disturbed and I, too, tried to keep it from him. When I explained that his father was a sick man, that he had an addiction which he could not control and that this was an illness which we all had to face and accept, it made an enormous difference to him. He was old enough to understand. I realised how understanding had helped me and thought it might help him also.'

We talked for half an hour and she promised to send me some explanatory literature. She also invited me to an Al-Anon meeting which was held regularly each week.

I read voraciously the pamphlets that Jill sent me, and a book on alcoholism which I had recently found, to my astonishment, in our bookshelves. This was the first indication I had that perhaps John himself realised that he was an alcoholic. I learnt, a long while after, that he had discovered it in the office which he had taken over and brought it home. He had not read it. The Al-Anon information gave me relief for it was stated, categorically, that alcoholism was an illness which no wife could be held responsible for inflicting. Many, many times, as I lay awake at night, I had wondered how I had caused my husband to become so estranged from me that he found nothing worth preserving in our relationship. To learn that I need not carry this heavy burden of guilt, that I was no more to blame than if he had tuberculosis or diabetes, was heartening. I also learnt that all my reactions were normal but wrong, that my natural anger assisted John in his need to project his own guilt and suffering on to me, that by behaving like a shrew I gave him justification for escaping into the haze of insensibility induced by the bottle. I discovered, too, that I was not helping him by trying to cover up the results of his drinking, that my connivance in attempting to reduce its effects on him simply compounded the weakness and increased the inevitability of its hold on him. I remembered how, when the wine merchant knocked at the door with a large, unpaid bill, I had in the past rushed to my cheque book and paid out the balance I was reserving for the rate demand or the electricity bill rather than have John faced with the shame of a summons; how, when he had blacked my eye in the first year of our marriage, I had immediately invented the story of walking into a door rather than admit the truth. I read that no amount of beseeching, as if I did not already know, was going to have any influence on his addiction.

In a muddled, intuitive way, I had already found that the best counter to John's attacks and to his apparent disregard for me was to create a life for myself independent of him, but I had not realised that by doing this I was not only able to be happy sometimes in my own world but that it also reduced his omnipotence over me, that by detaching myself from him I was also removing a support which he badly needed in order to retain his own self-respect and self-justification. As long as I continued to cling to him, and take the knocks for him, I lessened the chances of his seeing himself as he really was. His alcoholic *amour propre*, the illusions of importance that he maintained with the aid of drink, must not be supported but undermined through my refusal to accept anything but the truth. Love, without justice, cannot be maintained when the giving is one-sided and the giver resentful and bitter at the low return for outlay in thought and patience. Love becomes a duty, a chore, a burden, easily metamorphosed into hate, undisciplined and ambivalent.

I went to my first Al-Anon meeting and I was ashamed of my self-pity, for there I met others in far worse straits than myself, although I think, at that first opportunity to pour out all my pent-up woes to a circle of friendly, understanding, compassionate faces, I scarcely realised how fortunate I was. I still had a roof over my head, I had driven myself to the meeting in our own car, I had not suffered the indignities of the bailiff removing our furniture or the discomfort of the electricity board cutting off our supply of heat and light; John had not been in prison. Following this sense of shame came a bracing determination. I was inspired to see John in a new light, to separate the man I loved from the alcoholic I feared and despised, to accept that he was a sick man, that as I had no part in causing the sickness though considerable responsibility, in my ignorance, for nurturing and encouraging it, so I could not cure it. The message of Al-Anon is that, though it is impossible to change your alcoholic, it is possible to change yourself: take a good look at yourself and learn how to become whole again. In the process, if you are lucky, what you learn may rub off on those around you.

I returned home full of resolution—not to get angry, not to try to stop John drinking, not to allow anxiety to ruin my life, not to interfere with John's affairs in any way unless I felt that I must do so, on a practical level, for the sake of our children and myself. To some of these resolutions I adhered, with difficulty; anger, sometimes, in the face of almost overwhelming provocation, was a monstrous fiend to contain but I learned slowly how to avoid it. I quickly found it possible to restrain my urge to try, actively, to stop John drinking; I no longer begged him not to go out, knowing that it would be to the pub, or hid the bottles, but neither did I pretend that I did not know that he was drinking for that would have given him a false sense of security. But how could I avoid anxiety? I tried to squash it down, to ignore it, but if I would not acknowledge it in my mind, it forced itself into evidence through my body. I developed a recurrent backache and the pain mounting from the base of my spine would sometimes be the first indication I had that anxiety still had me in a vice-like grip: anxiety for the future, anxiety for the children, anxiety for my own sanity, and hatred for the man who caused such anxiety so persistently, debilitating my strength, decimating my energy. It is incredibly difficult to separate a person and love the good in him and feel compassion for the weak, when anxiety blinds the eyes and confuses the emotions.

Nevertheless, with the resurgence of confidence gained by the release from the guilt which had gnawed me for so long and made me uncertain of myself and vulnerable to John's jibes, and with a programme of steps I could take to improve the family situation, I was able to concentrate on considering each of the problems which confronted me and slowly establish a goal of stability for myself. My renewal of energy and decisiveness must have been apparent to John and it made him uneasy. A few days after my first contact with Al-Anon, he arrived home early, a mood of depression and self-pity engulfing him, apparent in his face and carriage. Although I felt a twinge of pity for him, I did not show any sympathy; nor did I feel resentment that he alone was responsible for the difficulties he caused and which he so often tried to blame on me. Alcoholism was an illness and I was willing to accept this without useless cavilling. If somebody is ill, there is usually some remedy or alleviation for their suffering; many of us prefer not to admit that we are sick, to run away from the knowledge out of fear of how fatally the canker may have eaten into us and how frightening the diagnosis and drastic the remedy may be. The desire to continue life as we know it, miserable though it is, rather than face a severe treatment the success of which we find it difficult to believe in and uncomfortable to undergo, makes cowards of us all. I felt that, having myself faced that John was suffering from a sickness which was, without doubt, progressive, I had to frighten him into realising this himself.

As he stood dejectedly in the kitchen reiterating that we would all be better off without him, that, if he died, we would have the insurance money and be able to lead a happy life (I did not know then that it was so long since the premiums had been paid that this was doubtful), I did not rise to the bait he usually so successfully held out to me. It was a ploy he frequently used when he had drunk himself into maudlinism, and my response was always to reassure him that we loved him, that we wanted him, if only he could stop behaving in such an impossible way so that we could not rely on him or believe what he said or lead a normal family life. He would gradually warm to my protestations of love and loyalty, promise to reform and life would be less fraught for a few days until, once again, his resolve crumbled and the alcohol took grip again. This time, I was untouched by his piteous search for sympathy. I did not hold him close and implicitly assure him that I would protect him by my devotion from the rigours of the world and the consequences of his own behaviour. Facing him across the kitchen table, I said firmly:

'You are not going to die tomorrow, or the next day, or even next year. You have an illness which may creep on for years and years, and it's going to get worse all the time. If you don't find help, your life is going to be degrading and horrible. You know that you can get help. You have only to lift the telephone and speak to Alcoholics Anonymous.'

I was amazed, and felt a wave of relief and hope when he said:

'All right. I'll telephone them. What's the number?'

An hour after he had spoken to Central Office, a local AA member telephoned him. He talked for a long time and I heard John protesting that really it was quite unnecessary for him to come and see him, he did not want to put him to such trouble, it was all rather silly really and he could manage; he had just been feeling depressed. Brian, his contact, ignored him and told him to keep off drink for the whole of the next day and he would come to our house in the evening.

John seemed both relieved and embarrassed: relieved that, at last, he had admitted to somebody that he knew he was sick, embarrassed that he was going to have to talk about himself. I felt overjoyed. Already I could see a new era before us.

Brian came the following evening and I think that John had avoided the temptation to drink that day. They talked for nearly four hours, and I pottered uselessly about the house, longing to hear what they were saying but controlling my urge to listen, aware that having accepted that I could not cure him I must not interfere when the work was begun by somebody else. When they finally emerged from their intense discussion, Brian looked at me and said:

'I think he's going to make it.'

I asked him if an alcoholic could drink at all.

'No,' he said definitely.

'Not even cider?' I asked.

'No.'

I was incredulous. I had associated alcoholism with the hard stuff, whisky, brandy and gin, for John had only become completely irrational when our income had begun to rise and he could afford spirits instead of beer. Certainly he had always been irresponsible, but he had kept his excesses within bounds. I found it difficult to believe that anybody could be affected by cider or beer in moderation. Those words 'in moderation' are the identification of the problem, for once the addiction is there, moderation is not possible. I do not know why this is but I do believe that it is. Neither, to my knowledge, has medical research yet produced an answer, only the observation that some people are subject to addiction while most are not. The question that at present defies solution is how to prevent addiction when it is only after it has occurred that the addict can be recognised. Much has been written about alcoholism over the past few years and it is more widely accepted as an illness now than it was that day, seven years ago, when I first stumbled to a realisation of what was wrong with my husband. Television presents programmes discussing the problem, newspapers publish reports of conferences on alcoholism, government now acknowledges the social implications of treating it as a crime rather than a disease, and magazines print articles on the recognition of the symptoms and the dangers of ignoring them. But, for many people, alcoholism is only associated with the down-and-out in Skid Row, clutching his bottle of meths; it is not something which can be related to the family disturbances carefully hidden behind the closed front doors and net curtains in suburbia, or the megalomanic behaviour in the boardroom. Everybody knows that old Bill drinks too much but he's a good fellow on the whole, and his wife is not easy to live with, poor old sod.

To live with an alcoholic without despair, it is essential that any doubt about the physiological origins of the addiction be ignored. Some people find it impossible to accept this, and are made bitter by the realisation that the bottle is more important than the happiness of the family, that apparently selfless love and support mean nothing against the pleasures of an evening in the pub with the boys. But Alcoholics Anonymous preaches that it is the *first* drink, after a period of abstinence, which does the damage, and I am sure they are right. An alcoholic may think he can control his drinking but his behaviour will be affected by it in a way that alcohol does not affect normal people and inevitably, finally, the alcohol will control him.

Fortunately I recognised the necessity of accepting that the addiction to drink was physiologically determined without demanding a precise explanation, for nobody could have given me one. And, by such acceptance, I saved myself the constant temptation to go back over the years and quantify the loss of joy in marital companionship, the material gains that had never come my way, the emotional satisfactions that eluded me. How can anyone feel bitterness towards a sick person? Towards life maybe, but I had always regarded life as a challenge, and now that the challenge was clearly defined, and I knew that my success in meeting it depended on my attitude towards it, the confusion which I had felt for so long no longer ruled. I could not change John but I could change myself and had only myself to blame if I did not succeed.

John went to an AA meeting the night after Brian's visit, and said that he was amazed by some of the stories he heard: that those people really knew what alcohol could do to a man. I felt hope soar: never before had he admitted that booze had anything to do with our problems.

We had been invited to dinner by a new acquaintance of mine at the end of that week and I arranged to meet John at the station in the car. Wondering whether he would be able to maintain his three-day-long abstinence in the face of the social drinking that was sure to occur, I leaned across and opened the car door. As he got in, smiling, the smell of beer hit me in the face; it was not strong, the odour did not emanate from his skin as it usually did, but there was no doubt it was there. I said nothing, not wishing to ruin the evening. We were offered sherry, and John accepted; there was wine at dinner, and though he only had one glass, which was unusual, I was conscious of every sip he took. I think it was the knowledge that he had succumbed, and that I knew it, that made his conversation a little irrational rather than the amount of alcohol he took, but our hosts did not notice. As he drove me home, I said little and felt the familiar fear that I always had when he was at the wheel.

So began three months of vacillation. For two more weeks he continued to go to work; sometimes he came home and went to an AA meeting but, after his initial enthusiasm, he became derogatory and called it the Band of Hope. Other times, he retired to bed, saying he was tired; whichever way it went, his attitude towards me was more guarded, he sought to rile me less, perhaps because he found there was no gain in it any more, that I no longer reacted to his attempted provocation. One thing I knew for certain: he was no longer enjoying his drinking, could not accuse me of exaggerating the effect it had on him and all the family; the pleasure that he had gained in the past from the companionship of his fellow drinkers was alloyed by the growing conviction that I was right, for now that the acknowledgement had come from him how could his protestations carry any true force? Evidence was building up against his recurrent attempts to persuade himself that he was not an alcoholic. One Saturday, he came home from his office after we had had our lunch, settled himself in front of the television screen and asked for his meal on a tray. He had clearly not been working much that morning. He made a clumsy attempt to show affection, calling me 'sweetie' which irritated me, for it was a term he only used when he was drunk. I had bought tickets for an open-air performance of a Shakespeare play, to which I had planned we should take the two older boys. I had learnt not to tell John of such arrangements until the time for departure drew near so as to avoid the chance of his spoiling the evening for the rest of us. If, when the time came, he was sober, we could include him in our outing and he would know that we liked to have him with us; if he had been drinking and was likely to spoil the event by his derogatory remarks, we would go by ourselves. Obviously that day he would be poor company. Because I had refrained from commenting on his condition he was friendly and, as I had no money left after my week-end shopping, I asked him if he had five shillings to buy the boys refreshments in the interval. He pulled three pound notes out of his pocket and said: 'Take these. I don't need them.' I accepted with the thought that we could now treat ourselves to supper in the marquee. John fell asleep in his chair and I gave the boys tea and arranged with my mother to put the little ones to bed for me. Michael and David were washing their faces and I was combing my hair when John came upstairs and said:

'By the way, I shall need the car this evening.'

Remembering that I had been advised that I should always try to outwit rather than argue with him, I said blandly:

'That's all right. I half expected you would if you knew we wanted it, so I've made other arrangements.'

This was a lie, and as I finished making up before my dressing-table mirror, my mind frantically searched for a solution. I didn't want to disappoint the boys. I thought of Diana and Bill up the road; they might be prepared to help me.

I went out and knocked on their door. Briefly I explained to them and asked if I could borrow their car. Not unnaturally, Bill was loathe to let me take it but said that he would drive us to our play, some ten miles away and inaccessible by public transport.

I protested that I could not let him do that, that I was sure I could think of something else and left them. As I reached our house, my brother-in-law was pulling into the kerb in his big family car. I leaned in through the window.

'Charles, hallo,' I said. 'You wouldn't, I suppose, let me borrow your mini tonight, would you? James and Michael and I have tickets for Polsden Lacey and John wants the car, which makes it a bit difficult, and I don't want to disappoint them.'

'You can't have the mini, because June is out in it,' said Charles. 'But you can take this if you like.'

'You're an angel,' I said. 'Are you quite sure? I've never driven a Rover before.'

'Of course,' he said. 'Go and get the boys and you can drive me home.'

Thanking God for such a generous brother-in-law, I rushed in to fetch the children, and we drove away. We all felt sad that, as so often, we were not going as a complete family but at least there was no tautness in the atmosphere and we enjoyed the play. When we arrived home very late, John was still up. I suspected that he had not been out at all. In our haste, we had left the dirty tea things, and John's lunch dishes, and the house had been in some slight disarray. Usually on these occasions, John made no attempt to clear up, but tonight the draining-board was empty and the rooms tidied. He asked us if we had enjoyed our evening. When the boys were getting ready for bed, John asked me if I had taken three pounds from his pocket. I said, incredulous: 'No, you gave it to me.'

'I didn't give it to you,' he said.

'Yes, you did. And Michael saw you do it. I'll go and fetch him.'

I called Michael who confirmed what I said.

John became silent, and then went to bed.

The next morning, he brought me up my breakfast before I was awake. This was not unusual; it was as though he sought by this indulgence to demonstrate his basic kindness which his actions so often belied. He sat on the bed and said that the event with the money had made him realise that he suffered from amnesia and that this convinced him that he really was an alcoholic. He had been fighting the knowledge, half admitting it but unable to accept the implications, refusing to believe that he really was like all those other people whom he had heard speak at AA meetings, with their declarations that their drinking had ruined other lives than their own; he had not wanted to be one of them, to declare his own guilt and bear the responsibility of his actions. He helped all that Sunday with the chores and tried to join in with the family activities, but he was quiet and withdrawn and in his eyes there was a bemused expression, as though for the first time he was allowing himself to see and was confused by what he saw. At the same time, there was a new determination about him; when the boys were noisy, I could see that although he was overcome with an exhaustion born of emotional and mental struggle, he controlled his usual reaction of irritation and did not turn upon them in anger. I determined that I must restrain my anxiety to help him, to push him the way I wanted him to go. I must cease to attempt to control him. I longed to use this moment of co-operation to draw him out, to discover the details of his indebtedness so that I could begin to plan the future. I knew that he had a bank overdraft and that the car was not paid for, and I suspected that his firm was heavily in debt. But my only comment was that, whatever trials he had to face, however we had to change our style of living in order to come to terms with our debts, I and the boys were with him; we only wished that we should lead a happy family life and, if we had to give up some material things, this was nothing set against the joy of reunion. I wanted to impress upon him a sense that he was loved and longed for him, in his turn, to confide in me his worries. But although he sought to please me in small ways, he seemed unable to understand or appreciate that, grateful though I was for the small domestic tasks he undertook and thankful that he appeared to notice that I was very tired, my great desire was to share with him: to share his fears and worries as well as his achievements.

When I said that I would come to the office again on Monday, he suggested that I should take a rest that week and I agreed, both because I needed the break and also because I did not want to give his partner the impression that I was interfering.

For two days he came home sober. But, on Wednesday, he was late and we had started dinner when he telephoned me from the station to ask me to fetch him. As we drove up the hill, he suggested that I was resentful at having had to interrupt my dinner, and my heart sank. It was the familiar provocation, the attempt to place me in the wrong, and I knew that he had again given way to his craving for alcohol.

The next evening, he was so obviously drunk that James and Michael realised at once. He laughed too much with the children and several times tried to alienate me with argumentative remarks. He said that a friend of his was arriving later and that he was going to drive him back to Bognor that night. I feared for his safety, and well aware that once the boys were in bed he would goad me further, I felt that I must remove myself. The exhaustion with which I lived, which was increased by the alternating hope inspired by John's apparent change of attitude and disappointment when I found it was so short-lived, made me weak in my determination to remain calm and detached and my instinct was to go out on these occasions. I was fortunate in my friends and there were several homes to which I could go to spend a relaxed evening until I had recovered my equilibrium. Being careful not to impose myself too often, I would distribute my impromptu visits, and at each house I was received without surprise and without comment, allowed to join the family in whatever they were doing, and would return fortified by a peaceful, unremarkable evening. When I arrived home at half-past eleven, all the downstairs lights were on, the curtains undrawn, and I saw John and his friend through the sitting-room window.

Hearing me come in, John came out into the hall, closing the door behind him.

'Where the devil have you been?' he said.

'I took my sewing to the Wilsons.'

'It was damned rude of you. Andy is here and he's staying the night, and you will give up your bed for him. And you will be pleasant to him as long as he's in my house.'

'I like Andy,' I said. 'Of course I'll be nice to him.'

I went upstairs to find some sheets to change the bed. John followed me.

'You are an abominable wife,' he shouted. As I passed the stairhead on my way to the spare room, I saw Andy slip out of the front door and wondered how much he knew.

When John discovered that his friend had gone, his anger mounted and his face became livid.

'None of my friends will ever come to the house again,' he cried out. 'It's a shameful thing when they have to leave because my wife comes home. Where are the car keys? I'll have to drive him to Bognor now.'

I gave them to him and he chased out of the house after Andy. Fearful of his driving capability, I prayed that they should have a safe journey, but he was back in a few minutes. In a furious voice, he ordered me to bed and went to his own room. I was interested to find the AA books and pamphlets which John had collected at the meetings he attended on my bedside table. Perhaps, in his befuddled state, he had decided that Andy needed help, that he was an alcoholic. I went straight to sleep.

John was still resentful the next morning, but went to London. He left the car keys at home, and aware that he might confiscate them from me after my behaviour of the night before, I ordered two more from the garage before fetching the boys from school. When we got home, John was sitting in the garden with his partner. I was shaking with nervousness when I realised the implications of this. During the week I had visited my doctor. I had been his patient since I was six and I knew him well. I felt that I must confide in him and get some tranquilliser pills to help me through the more difficult days with John. At his surgery, I was told that he was on holiday but that I could see his partner. She listened to me as I described our home life to her and my realisation that John was an alcoholic. She told me that she felt John's only hope was in Alcoholics Anonymous, that the failures of psychiatry and hospitalisation had been disheartening.

'You are obviously very fond of your husband,' she said.

'Yes,' I said. 'If only he could understand that,' and I felt my mouth tremble and my eyes fill with tears as I tried to control the emotion triggered by her understanding.

When I told her of my concern about John's business affairs she said that she thought I ought to tell his partner, and I had written him a long letter. He would have received it that morning. Now that I saw him in the garden with John, I was fearful of how he might react. Perhaps he was an alcoholic, too, for I could not understand how he could have been blind for so long to what had been evident to me as soon as I had started working at the office.

I made a pot of tea and carried it out into the garden. As I set the tray down on the grass, I glanced at George and knew that he was with me. John was looking nervous and embarrassed.

'John and I have been talking,' said George. 'I have told him that I think it would be a good idea if he had a couple of months at home. He tells me he is an alcoholic. He will have a better chance of fighting it if he isn't under pressure.'

He did not mention my letter.

'I think that's a very good idea,' I said.

John said nothing. He looked as though he had been drinking again, perhaps to give himself the courage to tell George.

In a few private moments, George warned me that the next few weeks were going to be very difficult. I assured him that I realised this but had fresh courage now that John seemed to be co-operating. I was ready to burst into tears of relief. If John had had the bravery to admit his alcoholism outside the closed community of fellow sufferers in AA, surely real progress was being made.

Chapter Five

As JOHN fought his lonely battle, I was coming to realise that much as I wished it he was not going to turn to me and pour out all his pain. I did not understand then how confused the mind of an alcoholic is. I realised that, behind the drinking, there must be some disturbance of the personality which had led to the driving need for the blessed release of alcohol, but I did not realise that the disturbance may be closely connected with his relationship with me, his wife. I had no conception of how an alcoholic can block out from consciousness much of what has occurred if it is repugnant to him and disturbs his peace of mind. I little realised that scenes that were remembered by me, detail by ugly detail, were erased from the memory of the alcoholic. I knew John, originally, as a cheerful, gregarious man, who could jolly me out of ill-temper, and charm me into seeing the rigours of living from his own happy-go-lucky viewpoint. As the years proceeded, the cheerfulness, the gregariousness and the charm were reserved for others, and I became the inquisitor and the judge, not an objective, dispassionate judge, but one whose life was affected by his ill-considered actions. His generosity to others caused deprivation to me; his lack of thought caused me hurt; his carelessness about conforming to a code of conduct which I believed essential in one's dealings with others disturbed the smooth passage of daily living which confused and enraged me. Since I was the one person who, day by day, was affected by his behaviour because of my dependency upon him, he could only regard me as his victim and his conscience. As his confessor, I was useless because he believed that I could only condemn. I dimly realised this and longed for him to find some compatible spirit in whom he would confide his inmost thoughts and fears.

The John who spent the next three months at home was lonely and withdrawn. Sometimes he would try to co-operate with the family and join in our life but always with a confused expression in his eyes, like a dog who desperately wants to please his master yet is fearful of his actions being misinterpreted and rebuked; there was none of the old spontaneity of enjoyment in him. He was conscious of being watched, guardedly, by the family, by my friends. Sometimes he would go out and come home manifestly drunk, and then I would withdraw. All joy had gone out of him. Slowly I began to realise that I had never really known my husband at all. I discovered that he was shy and lacking in self-confidence and I began to recognise him in David, our third son. David is a cheerful, open little boy, who delights others by his engagingly uncomplicated approach to life. If somebody is obviously unhappy, he is kind to them; if he is upset, he does not hide his feelings. With strangers he is shy and pushes his younger brother in front of him, and he hurts easily when people are unkind to him and shuts himself away, not understanding that much unkindness is unwitting. I realised that John must have been very similar to David when he was a child, and came to see that perhaps I had unintentionally caused him many hurts. With my capacity to protect myself and detach from those who gave me pain whilst wearing a friendly façade, I had lacked the perception to realise that John had never developed this skill. Like David, he could not simulate. Had he, therefore, even before I knew him, protected himself and his sensitivity with alcohol? Was, therefore, the man I thought I knew when I married him mainly the alcoholic man? Would he ever be able to live without that protection and talk openly about his feelings? I knew that somehow I had to show him that I was unimpressed with the aspirations and achievements of the alcoholic man but that I had love for and confidence in the real person, the man I scarcely knew. I must not try to delve into that person's feelings, I must not violate his privacy, I must wait and be patient and allow others, if he wished it, to be his confidants.

In the meantime, while John was grappling with the problem of his own personality, I decided it was my task to shoulder the more pressing everyday problems. I now received a weekly payment of ten pounds from the office which enabled me to pay for our weekly needs, but I had no clear idea of what our general financial position was. I telephoned the bank manager and asked if he would see me. He, too, had apparently been worried about John and endeavoured to talk some sense into him; he had, mercifully, refused to allow him any more credit. He told me that

John had nothing but an overdraft, agreed that I should sell the car and pay off the remainder of the money owed on it, paying the balance into the office account since it was owned by the business which was also severely in the red, but he insisted that the boys and I should not forego our summer holiday even though we could not afford it. He had not seen me for some time and expressed concern at how thin and strained I had become. I thought I could raise a personal loan from my parents which I could pay off in the autumn by working part-time. He showed his friendship and concern for John by suggesting that he should ask him to go sailing during the week. I was grateful for his calm appraisal of our situation, his restraint from commiseration for me, and his encouragement of my belief that John was going to pull through. Of the financial affairs of the business he told me little, but since this was no concern of mine I was content to remain ignorant.

The bank manager was not the first person in whom I confided. Once I had accepted that there was no virtue in the loyalty that I had imposed on myself to the alcoholic man, I knew that I must put my trust in other people, not indiscriminately, but at least in those whom I felt would give me emotional support. For years, my father and mother had lived in the flat at the top of our large house and we had not discussed John, although he had frequently accused me of going to them to talk about him. It was a great relief to be able to talk openly to my mother for I had kept her out of my life for too long. She had never interfered in the rows of which she could scarcely have been unconscious, for John never kept his voice down and if I closed a door in an attempt to prevent the worst quarrels from reaching the ears of my parents, he invariably threw it open again. It was remarkable that my mother had restrained herself for so many years from attempting to intervene when she was only too well, and unhappily, aware of the tension in the house. She did, it is true, relieve me when I was obviously exhausted by inviting the children upstairs so that I could rest, but she never made any criticism of John. Throughout my life I had insisted on my independence and she knew my obstinacy in admitting failure; wisely she did not drive me further from her by herself suggesting that something was seriously wrong with my marriage. My father would occasionally, when he came down to speak to me on some trivial matter, commiserate with me on my solitary evenings but I always countered his sympathy by insisting that I did not mind being alone and I do not think that he, absorbed as he was in his work, realised the extent of my solitude or was so attuned to the atmosphere of dissension as was my mother. I rarely spent an evening with them, perhaps because being unprepared to confide in them, I preferred not to have to maintain the front that I wore for them, and everybody else, for longer than was necessary to deflect sympathy. As the struggle against John's alcoholism proceeded, I began to keep my parents informed of each little step forward. They were concerned, compassionate, and, above all, practical. They eased for me the strain of the constant small chatter of the little boys by inviting them up to the flat, if I felt the need to escape for a while they were in the house as baby-sitters, and they showed their love by a complete lack of condemnation of John. My father, like the bank manager, thought to draw him out of himself by accompanying him on walks if he showed any desire for companionship. They readily advanced me the money for our holiday, although they themselves had little capital, saying that it was a gift which they did not expect to be repaid. Although I was glad of their involvement, I found, however, that it had its drawbacks. Struggling as I was to remain at all times outwardly calm and unperturbed, during both John's withdrawals and his recurrent drinking, the nervous strain that this self-discipline imposed began to show in my physical appearance. I was aware that my mother was worrying about me, and I found that it was more trying to be worried about than to do the worrying myself. When, in August, a long-projected move of my parents from the flat to a small bungalow some miles away became imminent, we all felt relieved.

Bill and Diana, our near neighbours, had long since accepted my need for understanding friends. I now turned to some other friends of mine from whom I had always hidden my marital unhappiness. I telephoned Pamela Wilson and asked her whether I could come and talk to her and her husband, Kenneth. I had known Pamela since our eldest boys started at preparatory school six years previously. With children of the same age, Pamela and I developed a friendship, took it in turns to have each other's children when one of us wanted a free day, and Kenneth and John came to know each other. They did not have a lot in common but were well acquainted through the boys. Pamela and I sometimes took a day off together when all the boys were at school, and went for long walks in the country. We talked of the children, the problems of being housebound wives who felt the urge to extend ourselves beyond domesticity but rarely of our husbands. When John passed his final examinations, we went to dinner with the Wilsons and they were warmly glad for us. Pamela knew that John frequently came home very late but I had given the impression that this was due to extreme pressure of work. She was a reserved woman, with no propensity to gossip but with a thoughtful intelligence which enabled her to listen and evaluate without glib commitment or condemnation. She appeared to have none of my unpredictable swings of mood from high elation to hopeless despair.

I had always admired Kenneth who seemed to me, compared with John, to be an excellent husband and father. He took his wife out so that she was included in his life, he gave his sons attention and shared with them in their pastimes, his life seemed well-ordered and content. John could not help being conscious that Kenneth, to me, fitted my idea of a husband in a way that he himself sadly failed to fulfil. To my surprise, I had recently heard from Pamela that Kenneth was giving up, with her full support and encouragement, the safe, well-paid job he had with a large organisation because he felt ill-suited to it, that he must find work which gave him a sense of fulfilment before he was too old to change. This decision increased them both in my esteem. I admired Kenneth for the courage which enabled him to change the course of his life in middle-age and risk considerable loss of income, and Pamela for her understanding co-operation.

When I arrived at their home, they welcomed me with coffee and their full attention. I sat opposite them both at their kitchen table and said, without preamble:

'Do you know that John is an alcoholic?'

Pamela looked at Kenneth.

'We had begun to wonder,' she said. 'We met him in the buffet when we were coming down from London on Saturday morning, and it was obvious that he had already had a drink or two even though it was only midday.'

Without horror, or disbelief that this should happen to our sort of people, they gave me a sense of being ready to involve themselves in any way they could that might help. I explained to them what I had learnt from Al-Anon, and was assured that at any time I needed relief from the strain of living in the tense atmosphere that pervaded our home, I would always be welcome.

Kenneth suggested that John might like to play a round of golf with him: since his life, also, was in a state of flux and because, having broken from his past environment, he also felt a sense of isolation which might help John to identify a little with him, there might be a chance that John would be able to talk to him in a way that his own isolation and feeling of not being normal prevented with most people who were still on the treadmill. This compassionate consideration made me weep with the relief of unburdening long-suppressed unhappiness; it was good to know that here were two friends before whom I need no longer wear a mask. I had exposed my bitterness at my first Al-Anon meeting, shedding most of it on to those anonymous people who could accept it because they too had suffered the same crippling emotions. To the Wilsons, who were my friends, I only wished to show the unhappiness, not of myself alone but of John too, which lay behind the façade of normality, and the determination to face the truth and to try to get John to face it too.

I was astonished to find how, in the face of a straightforward, unlamenting statement of our condition, so many people responded. I had been worried for some time by the effect on Michael of John's behaviour and the nervous tension which caused me to be irritable and sometimes unfairly angered by the boys. There was an atmosphere of unease and tautness in the house which must have given both him and James a sense of foreboding when they returned home from school. David and Andrew were too young to be fully aware of it, and were usually asleep when their father came home. After I had bathed them and put them to bed, I would go downstairs and find my nervous expectation of what the evening would bring made it impossible for me to be relaxed with the older ones. I had always tried to hide from them the bitterness which existed between John and myself but, though I tried to disguise my fear, the symptoms of it were in my inability to deal gently and calmly with any small upset which might occur between them. James found solace in his books and usually retired to his room, but Michael was a more extrovert boy who liked to share his life with others. He seemed to be more perceptive than James, picking up nuances of meaning in a remark from John which appeared to escape James. Perhaps James simply cut off. Anxious, as I myself was, for his relationships with others to be smooth and uncomplicated, he must have found the phenomena of the swings of moods and behaviour from his father, sometimes excessively loving, sometimes incomprehensibly excluding, difficult. He was concerned to please and frequently helped me when he realised how tired I was. But the uncertainty of the warmth and sanctuary that he should have been able to expect in his own home, and the effort which he put in trying to contribute to it, took its toll on him. One day, while I was still going to John's office and facing my own despair at what I found, I had as usual fetched David and Andrew from school and was getting the boys' tea ready when Michael came in. He dumped his satchel on the floor and made a cheery remark to the little boys. Then a schoolfriend from along the road followed him in through the back door. We had known him since he and Michael were babies and we treated him as one of the family.

'Hello,' he said to Michael. 'Why weren't you at school to-day?'

'He was,' I said.

'Oh,' said the friend. 'I didn't see him, and I thought he must be ill.'

Michael looked a little confused, and agreed that he had not seen his friend either.

I said nothing until after the boy had gone.

'Weren't you at school to-day, Michael?' I asked.

'No,' he said flatly.

'Where were you?'

'I stayed in the park all day.'

'Why?'

'I don't know,' he said. 'I couldn't go to school.'

'What did you do? Did you have any lunch?'

'No. I just walked around a bit, and lay on the grass until it was time to come home.'

'Oh, Michael,' I said. 'Why did you do that? Are you unhappy?'

'Yes,' he said, and he began crying.

I thought for a moment.

'Is it because of Daddy?' I asked.

'Yes. Everything seems to be wrong, and you are always unhappy, and I try to pretend all the time that it's all right, but it isn't,' he sobbed.

I held him to me and stroked his head. I imagined the poor little boy filling in the long hours of that day, knowing he ought to be at school, too confused to understand that he, too, had been wearing a false face to hide from the world his misery, and unable at last to keep it up any longer. He was, after all, only eleven. Jill was right. He must be told of his father's sickness.

When he was in bed that night, slightly comforted because I had not been angry with him, I went to him.

'Michael,' I said. 'Do you know that Daddy is a sick man?'

'No,' he said. 'How?'

'Well, you know how he gets angry and loses his temper and then we all get upset. It isn't his fault. He has an illness which makes him drink and this makes him behave the way he does. Do you think you can try to understand that he is ill and cannot help his drinking? I didn't understand this myself until very recently, but now I do and I am trying to think how we can help him get better. That's why I went out last Tuesday evening. I'm trying to learn more about it and to persuade him that he can be cured if only he can understand himself that he is ill. Now we know, we can love him and try not to be too upset by his behaviour. Do you think you can do that? To know that he really is a kind and loving man who is sick?'

'I'll try,' said Michael.

'And I'll try, too,' I said. 'I haven't helped you, have I, by being bad-tempered so often. Let's both try.'

'What about school.?'

'Tomorrow I will go and see your headmaster and explain to him. You won't get into trouble.'

'That's good.'

'Will you sleep now?'

'Yes. I think I will.'

The same evening, I told James also. He did not seem very interested. I gave him a pamphlet on alcoholism to read; it always seemed more successful to approach James through his intellect than his emotions. I think he read it. I learnt later that he had confided in his friend at school and perhaps this relieved him for he certainly appeared to make a great effort to ease the tensions at home which, before, he had tended to aggravate.

As I had promised Michael, I telephoned his headmaster and made an appointment to see him. I felt a little nervous, not of his reaction but of my ability to tell my story dispassionately so as not to excite his sympathy for me and so evoke my tears. I had already learnt that sympathy was intolerable, reducing my ability to keep my mind on a practical plane and my emotions uninvolved. Having at last understood the futility of self-pity, I wanted none of it and in my effort to avoid it I adopted a shell of hard utilitarianism.

'Do you mind if I smoke?' I asked, as he welcomed me into his study.

'No, of course not,' he said. He looked vaguely round for an ash tray and then handed me a glass. 'Can you manage with that?'

'Did you know Michael was away from school yesterday?'

'Yes.'

'He played truant. I believe he has also had some trouble with his exercise books, saying they have been stolen or torn up. I think, perhaps, he may have done it himself.'

'Yes?'

'John is an alcoholic. I've only fully understood this myself lately. As you can imagine, our home life isn't very happy, and I believe Michael has been more affected than I realised. Will you please overlook his truancy?'

The headmaster shifted his chair slightly.

'I'm glad you've come to see me,' he said. 'We have been a little worried about Michael recently and I was going to ask you if there was anything wrong at home. Obviously, now I know, he will not be punished for his behaviour. And we will watch him carefully. Can I be of help in any other way? What about David and Andrew?'

'I think they are too young to be much aware at present,' I said. 'We are hoping that, now we recognise it for what it is, John will be able to recover. But there's no certainty. We might have to take them all away from the school. Would you be prepared to waive the term's notice if we can't keep them here after this term?'

'I'm sure that can be arranged. But I'll have to speak to the Board. I am not responsible for the school's financial affairs, you understand.'

'Yes. Would it be a good idea if I went to see Mr. James?'

Alastair James was a member of the school Board with whom I had a slight acquaintance.

'I think it would be a very good idea,' said the headmaster. 'I'm sure you'll find him very helpful.'

It had been easy. I was glad that I had decided to be completely honest.

The next week I visited Alastair James. He too listened to my story.

'John's an alcoholic? Well,' he said. 'I came down on the train with him the other day, and we had a drink together. I had no idea. I am sorry.'

He promised that we should not have to pay fees in lieu of notice and said that he did not think it would be necessary for him to tell the Board the complete truth.

'You won't mind if I tell Jennie, will you?' he asked. 'We always tell each other everything and she is completely trustworthy.'

'No, of course not,' I said. How wonderful, I thought, to have a relationship with your wife where you share everything.

'You're a plucky girl,' said Alastair, as he showed me out. 'Do you know, I have always thought of you as a well-conducted young woman.'

I felt a delightful glow of pleasure, and a gleeful sense that that was the most charming, old-fashioned compliment I had ever had. 'A well-conducted young woman!' Alastair had never seen me in my own home, shrieking uncontrollably at John.

I paid the next term's fees out of money I borrowed from another friend against a small security I held, anxious to hang on and allow the boys' education to continue undisturbed until I was certain that John's recovery was not going to come in the foreseeable future. By the end of the autumn term, though, I knew that we would have to move them to non-fee paying schools. I telephoned the headmaster and told him that they would have to leave. Three days later, he telephoned me to say that somebody who wished to remain anonymous had expressed a desire to help any boy in the school whose parents were unable to keep him there because of financial difficulties. I felt like the heroine in *Daddy Longlegs*, although I knew that it was for the boy's sake that this benevolence was being bestowed. Michael, at least, was safe for the next two years. Still unwilling to disturb David and Andrew until I was certain it was going to be necessary, I arranged with Alastair James that they could stay at the school until the end of the academic year if I undertook to pay the fees in instalments extending over the following two years should it prove necessary to remove them. It was less my doubt about the adequacy of the local state school, for by now a new infant school had been built and I had heard good reports of it, than my anxiety that, with their home life uncertainly stable, they should not be exposed to further upset by changing schools, which caused me to take on this financial responsibility.

James had taken a long time to settle down happily at his public day school and I knew that he would be extremely distressed if he had to leave now. Although he was withdrawn at home, he had found a niche for himself at school, had made a close friend in whom he found comfort and support, and preferred the school terms to the holidays. I went to see his headmaster and was passed on to the person responsible to the Governors for the financial affairs of the school. Once again, I found understanding and support in my belief that it might do irreparable harm to James if he were taken away at the age of thirteen, and the fees were waived term by term as our financial situation worsened.

Having dealt with the security of the boys for the time being, I was greatly relieved by the removal of this overriding worry. The summer holidays came and they were strangely languorous. With John at home, there was no reason for us to rise early. We now slept permanently in separate rooms and, if the day before had been trying, although I always woke early I would lie in bed reading in an attempt to conserve my energy rather than throw myself out of bed before I was properly awake in order to forestall the familiar constriction which gripped my stomach the moment I emerged properly from unconsciousness. Although I attempted not to, I was constantly watching John and was aware of his slightest change of mood. On good days, he would go out and spend his time gardening; but sometimes I would suddenly realise that he was no longer there. He had slipped out for a stealthy drink, hoping to be back before I noticed his absence. I learnt where to find the empty bottles which he attempted to hide from me, under the bed, behind the clothes in the wardrobe, beneath the upturned wheelbarrow, and would remove them to the dustbin. When he later found them gone, he would once again know that I was not deceived by his ostentatious display of abstention from drink. I believed he had a stock of wine in his closed local office and I knew that he had a large reserve being held for him by the wine-merchant. Each time he realised that I was not fooled, he would attempt to provoke me into anger. I asked him one night why he hated me so much.

'Because you are taking away my self-respect,' he said. 'But I am going to destroy you, too.'

'You can't do that,' I said. 'I know now that you are not mad or wicked, but sick. I want to help you because I love you.'

'Nonsense,' he said. 'I've been thinking about it and I believe that I am essentially evil.'

'No. It's the booze that brings out the bad side of you, but I am sure that the power of good is stronger than the power of evil, and I shall not give up.'

'That's all claptrap, and I shall prove it.'

I smiled. 'I still love you.'

I was determined that he should know that he was not alone although he seemed unable to accept my assurance. He was determined to cut himself off from us as though to punish himself the more, and to punish us for appearing to be happy. Sometimes he would say he preferred not to eat with us, and cook his own meals and take them to his room. Michael began to grow touchy, but he and James were going to stay with my brother and his wife for a few days and I hoped that removal from this unnatural atmosphere would relax him and that he would be able to enjoy himself for a little while. Although it was better now that James and Michael knew the reason for their father's strange behaviour because we were able to talk about it, and they too learnt not to react spontaneously to his anger or goading but maintained a forced lightness or quickly removed themselves from a difficult situation, their knowledge caused John to needle them as well as me for he realised that he could no longer hide from them his addiction. Only David and Andrew escaped his tauntings or his sullenness for they gave him their love without a guarded reserve and he began to lean on their childish uncritical affection. There were days when John tried, after suffering his self-imposed isolation from the family, to join with us in our activities but always there were sudden irrational changes of mood. One morning we all decided to have a day out walking in the country. John had said that he was going to his local office to start clearing it of files. We met him mid-morning and drove out to the Downs. Although immediately he joined us I knew that he had been drinking, I tried not to show it and the walk started well. After a picnic lunch we began crossing a golf course. Suddenly John complained that we should not be walking over the course, that if any of the members saw us he would be banned from his club, that it was a heinous crime that we were committing. The change of mood was so unexpected that I made the mistake of arguing that he was being absurd. He turned upon me and began accusing me of trying to ruin his life. In my disappointment that yet another day was spoilt, I burst into tears. David, ever sensitive to the unhappiness of others, began crying too, and then so did little Andrew. We were a pitiable sight as we sniffled our way along. Within half an hour, John's rage subsided and he lay down in the sun and fell into a deep, snoring sleep. I recovered myself, apologised to the boys for my lack of control, assured the little ones that all was well but Daddy was tired, and we amused ourselves until he woke an hour or so later. I was always amazed by his ability to fall asleep after a scene which shredded my nerves.

When James and Michael went away, I decided that I must spend a couple of nights away myself and asked Pamela and Kenneth if I could stay with them. I had no fear for the two small boys for I knew that John would care for them and be kind to them. I was very conscious that when he was alone with them they all enjoyed themselves. John agreed that I needed a rest; he seemed strangely aware of the strain he was putting upon me and part of him, the part which I clung to as the real John, showed concern for me. He drove me to the Wilsons and, as he handed me over at the door, also produced a large bottle of wine as a gift for the Wilsons. Kenneth, believing he had stopped drinking, was touched by his thought, and we all agreed hopefully that perhaps he was anxious to get rid of the temptation which constantly nagged him. The Wilsons were kind and thoughtful, we talked little of John and my problems.

They drove me home two days later, feeling refreshed and a little apprehensive. John and David and Andrew welcomed me at the door, the boys exuberant in their greetings, John tepid but not unfriendly. I learnt that, while I had been away, he had talked to his partner who was anxious that he should go to a psychiatrist. The professional association to which John belonged had been obliged to investigate some complaints they had received about him, and it was important for the business that John should receive a medical opinion on his condition. He had written to our doctor and told me that he supposed it would end up with his having to see a 'headshrinker'. I had so longed for him to seek help and advice that I was delighted that circumstances had finally pushed him into doing something about it; that he himself had volunteered the information to me was even more cheering. There was so little contact between us.

There were nights when I felt so lonely, so bereft of love, that I would creep into John's room and bed to be enfolded by his sleepy, semi-conscious warmth. There were mornings when I awoke to find John beside me in my bed. Then we would be happy for a little while until once again the draw of the bottle overwhelmed him. There were other nights when he would come in after an evening's absence, the sweet pervading smell of whisky unmistakably tainting the air around him, and attempt to hold and fondle me, only to be rebuffed. I detested the dampness of his skin then, and the grossness of his body. He would quickly turn sour at my distaste for him and lash me with his tongue. 'Cold bitch,' he would mutter as he pushed me away. If he left me, I would untense my muscles and turn over, grateful for the cool solitude of my bed; sometimes he did not leave me but would push me out on to the floor and stand over me expressing his contempt for me and his hatred of my relentless rejection of him and his virility, a virility which I knew could be promising in intention but peter away before its climax. I knew that he could still arouse my sexuality, even when drunk, but I also knew that it was I who would be left to toss and turn in frustrated desire throughout the night, denied the pleasure of fulfilment, while he subsided into noisy oblivion, his heavy breathing stertorous and mocking in its indifference to me. I no longer cared to expose myself to this pain, which reduced my ability to remain detached; it was preferable to suffer the injustice of being accused of frigidity for this I could wear as a sheath of emotional impenetrability.

One night I woke myself up, sobbing. I had dreamt that I was surrounded by John's friends who were all jeering at me, shouting and laughing about John's mistresses; they would not stop, they taunted me with their knowledge and they hemmed me in so that I could not escape from their loathsome enjoyment of my misery. They insisted that I listened. I ran, still sobbing, to John's room and he woke immediately and came back to my bed to comfort me. I told him of my dream and that I now realised that I must face the fact that he may have turned to other women in his loneliness, and he held me tight and told me that he loved me. He said that he did not want to be alone any more, that he could not be alone any more; soothed by his assurances, relieved to push my fear from me, I went to sleep.

We did not speak of the dream again.

A few days later, while John was out, a woman telephoned and asked for him. She did not leave her name but said she would telephone again. Whilst I was getting lunch, I felt fear clench my stomach again. I had forgotten my nightmare but now it returned to me. Was John, even now, going to some other woman? The name 'Angela' kept running through my mind. I had seen it written in John's handwriting on a piece of paper on the desk, above some curious, meaningless message, and had dismissed it as a piece of nonsense written while his mind was clouded. Now I began to feel certain that this gripping fear was based in reality, was not wrought out of an over-active imagination. Was it 'Angela' who had rung? John did not come home for lunch but I had become accustomed to his unexplained absences and gave David and Andrew their meal without comment. While I washed up, I felt a physical sickness in my stomach. I gathered the boys and their windcheaters and the dog into the car and we drove to collect two of their friends who had been invited to tea. I took them all to the park for a while, hoping that they would exhaust themselves through their games, for their exuberance was rasping on my sensitive nerves. As they ran off, I collapsed on to the grass and lay on my back, my face to the open, uncluttered sky. I felt the need for space, to push away all the impinging responsibilities of children, the crowding in of people I had to see, of things I had to do; I had to think my way through this new fear.

I prayed: 'God give me strength. Give me strength to let go, to let go not only of my efforts to push John into finding his way back to peace and stability, but to let go of John, with love, to another woman if this will help him.'

I believe I was sincere. When I felt I had mastered my panic, I called the children and we walked back to the car. On our way, we passed a dog trying to mount a bitch.

'What are those dogs doing, Mummy?' asked Andrew, interested. 'Are they trying to make babies?'

I felt faint at the sight. Was John with 'Angela' now, flesh against bare flesh, limb locked with limb?

As we drove home, the boys shouting with high spirits in the back of the car, I repeated to myself: 'God, give me courage. God, give me courage.'

We came into the kitchen through the back door, and I saw that John's lunch place was still laid untouched, on the table.

Then, with a great surge of relief, I saw that his food had been taken from the oven. I went along the passage and from the foot of the stairs I saw his back as he went into his room. I rushed upstairs and cried: 'Thank goodness you are here. Thank goodness.'

Although he was drunk, he was concerned for a moment. He held me to him and said: 'Hey, now, what's the matter? What's the matter?'

I leaned against his chest and could not speak.

When I had stopped trembling, I told him that I would tell him later, that I had to get tea for the children. He lost interest and turned away.

He came down to the playroom while the boys were having their tea. He must have drunk more since I left him for he wore the idiotic simper which he often adopted when he was trying to appear normal and friendly. Quietly, in the kitchen so that the boys should not hear from the adjoining room, I told him that I did know that he was drinking. Immediately his expression changed to one of hostility and he began making menacing threats in an undertone.

'Please don't spoil the homecoming for James and Michael,' I said. The two older boys were expected that night. John left me then and played boisterously with the children, and I went up to his room. There was an empty bottle of whisky in the poacher's pocket he had had made in the inside of his sports jacket, and there were three bottles of wine in his wardrobe behind the clothes. I took the young friends home and stayed out for a while to enable John to have time to sober up a little. Once I had made it clear that he was not deceiving me in his drinking, I usually found that he stopped for a while provided that I did not labour the point. I never, now, asked him not to drink. I called in on the doctor, who told me he had received John's letter.

'Did you know that I came to see you while you were away? Had you realised John was an alcoholic?'

'Yes, dear,' he said.

'How long have you known?'

'For a long time.'

'Why didn't you tell me?'

'There was no point. You can't do anything.'

Then, I felt he was right. I had learnt the hard way that I couldn't do anything; perhaps he wished me to be spared the knowledge for as long as possible. Now, I think he was wrong. If I had known, I would have found out more about it and at least not have had to suffer the uncertainty about my own sanity. Already, with a little knowledge, I was able to make slow progress on myself at least. Ignorance causes fear of the unknown, and there is no worse fear for it is a constant threat which, being unidentifiable, is unassailable. With knowledge, I could forge for myself the armour and the weapons to protect myself from fear and slowly build my own foundation of stability on which the children could rely.

Now that John himself had written to him, the doctor promised to do what he could. We arranged that I would telephone him when I was sure that John was sober, for there was no point in his seeing him when his mind was fogged with alcohol and he lied with ease and conviction.

John was out when I got home and still away when James and Michael arrived, full of enthusiasm for their visit to my brother and looking more relaxed than they had for several weeks. When John came back, he was pleasant and friendly to all of us.

The doctor came the next morning, straight after my early call to his surgery. He arranged for John to see a psychiatrist. I was pleased. It seemed another step forward. John, too, though grudgingly, appeared to be glad that circumstances were forcing him to seek help and advice. I took the risk, while his mood was amenable, of suggesting that we would have to sell the car; finding that this did not throw him out of countenance, I dared also to propose that, when my parents moved in the next few weeks, we should find tenants for the flat. I knew that he might be resistant to these unpleasant necessities and that the usual reaction to having them forced upon him of, first, withdrawal, then another bout of heavy drinking and attempted provocation would probably follow, but I had learnt that once we had been through this predictable sequence of responses I had usually gained a little ground. The ignominy and last despairing rebuttal of defeat, as he saw the edifice of an illusory material security being destroyed, brick by brick, waned to lethargy. I had to plan for our economic survival, but I had no wish to do so without informing him of each decision to be made, in the faint hope that he might even co-operate in the planning.

All the wine in his cupboard had gone by lunchtime the

following day. John already plastered, I felt that I could lose nothing by forcing a few more facts into the open and told him that I realised that he had a hoard of wine stashed away somewhere. He was furious with me and ate his lunch in silence. The boys behaved sensibly and we managed to maintain some conversation. John refused pudding, saying that since I seemed to think that I was supporting the family he had better do the washing-up. I did not argue. I knew that by excluding John when he was in this mood and giving the impression that we could enjoy ourselves without him, we drew him back into the family sooner, for the greater his sense of isolation the greater his need for our companionship became and the shorter the bouts of drinking with which he cut himself off from us. But, though the boys played the game with me of pretending that we were vastly merry, they could not know why I played it and it was a hard game. By the evening, Michael was again looking strained. My brother and his wife, who had brought them home, had spent the day with my parents. On their suggestion he returned home with them until the time came for us to go away on holiday.

Al-Anon had taught me not to prop the alcoholic up. Love is not possible without justice and I must not allow my desire for peace make me give way to the wish of the alcoholic to avoid responsibility. I hoped that I was treading this delicate path wisely for I could understand the sense of it. John no longer maintained contact with Alcoholics Anonymous; I was told that he would go to them when he was ready, when he had reached his rock bottom. Until he went voluntarily, they could not help him. Rock bottom, I was assured, did not always mean Skid Row. Each man had his own lowest level of endurance and many find it before they lose everything. I was conscious that, even if I withdrew my support, I could not withdraw that of the younger children. I had tried to explain the policy of separation of the dual personality of the alcoholic to James and Michael, but it was hard for them to understand. Detachment too closely resembles unfeeling cruelty. James, outwardly, detached himself from all of us, but Michael's friendly heart found the pain too much. I knew that only by removal from home could he get through the next few weeks of the holidays without anguish, for at home he could not avoid close contact with the unhappy climate invoked by his father's emotional separation from us all. He was fond of my brother and happy to go away again and, having the distress he felt for John in his solitude removed from my direct consciousness, made it less difficult for me to remain firm in resolution.

David and Andrew were unaware and therefore their attachment to their father was untarnished by doubt and the condemnation he felt implicit in the attitude the rest of us adopted, incapable as he was of grasping the underlying love which compelled our actions. Drunk or sober, his relationship with them was straightforward and they accepted him as he was. He was more fun than I, he played with them more, and when he was bad-tempered he did not try to hurt them by innuendo or direct attack as he did the older boys and myself. Being young, they lived in the present and did not anticipate tomorrow. I had no fear for them when I left them with him for I knew he would be kind to them: he needed their unquestioning affection. They had been less conscious than their brothers of my instability for, in the past, our rows had been in the evening after they were asleep; they had not heard his worst excesses of anger or my anguished sobbing. Now that he was at home all day, the rows had ceased because I had learnt control. Unable to provoke me, John usually retreated defeated to his room, and they only knew that Daddy was tired.

There were days when I myself found detachment inhumanly demanding. The forlorn, hurt look in John's eyes sometimes tore at me. One morning I picked some flowers from the garden and put them in his room. This small act of love seemed to draw a response for, soon afterwards, I heard him singing and he appeared happy for a few hours.

There were times, however, when I outreached myself in my attempt to outwit and keep a step ahead of John, when the game became fun to play and my attitude towards him callous. One night, when he was out and I was feeling low in spirit, I took the dog for his usual cigarette-buying walk. I was wearing old jeans, and as I strolled down the road, I felt my car keys in the pocket. I reached the station and, just as I was turning back home with my cigarettes, I saw our car parked down the road, outside the entrance to a basement drinking club. Seized by impulse which I rationalised to myself as having been impelled by the fear that John, in his inevitable inebriation, might crash the car on his way home, I unlocked the door and got in. I drove home, parked the car in the garage which we rented further up the road and walked back to the house. I was feeling slightly exhilarated. I persuaded myself that fate had willed this event for I rarely carried my keys in my pocket, usually hanging them on a hook in the kitchen as I came in. It was not until I was sitting innocently in the drawing-room with my mending that I realised the iniquity of what I had done. To calm my apprehension of what John would do when he discovered the loss, I turned on the television and watched a play, trying to ignore the frightened pulsing of my heart. The telephone rang just as the play ended. John was speaking from the police station.

'Have you got the car?' he said.

'No,' I lied. 'I thought you had it.'

'It appears to have been stolen. I've got to give the registration details to the police. Could you find the logbook?'

Whilst I was looking for it, I thought quickly.

Picking up the telephone receiver again, I began giving the details to John, then suggested that I should speak to the policeman and give him them direct; it would be simpler.

'Yes, madam?' the calm voice of the policeman gave me courage.

'Can my husband hear what I am saying?'

'No.'

'Then I must tell you that the car is in the garage. My husband is an alcoholic and suffers from amnesia. This is very confidential so please don't say anything to him. I will come and see you tomorrow to explain.'

'Very well, madam,' he said.

I put down the telephone and went into the kitchen to make some coffee. It would not be difficult for me to appear concerned about the loss of the car, for I was terrified by what I had done and had no need to feign agitation. A few minutes later, John came in, his whole bearing expressive of his drunken rage at 'the swine who had stolen the car'. I breathed with relief that he did not appear to suspect me. He went into the drawing-room and subsided in front of the TV screen. Within moments, he appeared to have forgotten the whole matter.

The next morning, early, an old friend of his called upon him whilst he was still asleep. I had been to several of his own friends as well as mine in the hope that they might be able to help him, and they all expressed their desire to co-operate. I took the man up to John's room, and as I followed him up the stairs I smelt the drink in him. I realised then that he was unlikely to be of much assistance, and when he came down later to wait for John whilst he dressed and sat at the kitchen table talking to me, I suspected that he was an alcoholic himself. He and John were going out to follow a golf match round the course; he assured me that he would not take John near a pub. When John came down, he seemed surprised that his own friends knew of his alcoholism, but not resentful. As they went out, he said that if the headshrinker telephoned I could make an appointment. I told him that I already had but did not intend to tell him when it was in case he jibbed at the last moment. He made no mention of the car. Through the morning, I worried about my prank of the night before; it had been a sick joke. The more I thought, the less convinced I became that John would believe that he had had amnesia and the less I cared for carrying on the deception. It did not seem wise or worthy to adopt for myself John's practice of lying his way through a difficult situation. I decided that I must be honest with both the police and with John. I drove to the police station and asked for the station sergeant. He was a kindly man and listened quietly while I told him the story. He agreed that I must tell John the truth. When I got home, I left the car outside the house.

John came back soon after me. He smelt of beer but was not very drunk. He asked how the car had been returned. Calmly, I told him that it had been in the garage when he telephoned since I myself had brought it home, that the police knew, so there was nothing to worry about. He grunted and said no more. He attached little importance to the whole affair.

It struck me again and again how right my new attitude of avoiding secretiveness was. Indiscriminate publicity of John's illness would have been unkind and unnecessary, but now that the people we knew well were aware of his addiction, he could not charm them into reflecting back to him his own illusory assessment of himself. Unable to rely upon their connivance in supporting his fantasy that he was a normal, unafflicted man, with a neurotic wife who undermined his efforts to succeed in the world and made his home life uneasy with her accusations, he began to evince an uneasy acknowledgement that perhaps he must accept help. Michael's unhappiness had affected him too; when I told him that I had found the boy in his room the day after he came home from his visit, weeping because he thought his father was going to die, he was deeply shaken and had not sought to prevent him returning to my brother's home.

When the psychiatrist came to see John, I did not attend the interview, or even see the man. John told me afterwards that he had said that he should think about treatment in hospital and that, if he was willing to enter as a voluntary patient, he would be accepted. He was horrified by the thought of entering a mental hospital and vacillated between grim acceptance of the necessity and scoffing rejection of all psychiatrists and their absurd quackish notions.

We suffered the uncertainty of the following weeks with the accustomed pattern of heavy drinking followed by short periods of sullen sobriety, lightened from time to time by determined efforts by John not to allow his moods to impinge upon the family. Increasingly I was finding that the need to remain impassive and detached whatever the situation took a great toll upon my body and I was exhausted by the smallest physical tasks. John would still attempt violence at times, in an effort to produce some reaction. But I had found a new strength. For years, I had regarded religion with some scepticism, believing it the refuge of the weak, the straw to which the drowning man clings. Through my attendance at Al-Anon meetings, I had learnt the strength of faith, not in the dogmatised beliefs of the established Church, but in the power of good and the acceptance of a power greater than myself. I frequently prayed to my indeterminate God. I developed the habit of slipping to my knees whenever John went out, to pray for him, that he should be safe, that he should become aware of this power of good and cease to fight against life. In my lowest, most despairing moods, for myself not for John, when I felt that I was using the last reserves of that pool of energy which I needed to maintain my equilibrium and that soon I must surely break, I found that I could restore myself and replenish the pool simply by playing a beautiful record that we had of Handel's *Messiah.* As soon as Schwarzkopf's clear, pure voice swept out with the words, 'Come unto him, all ye that are heavy laden; take his yolk upon you and he will give you peace,' I knew that it was true; I wept gently to myself as I listened to the breathless perfection of her rendering and regained my sanity. For the first time, I understood the anguish of accepting the burden and the peace of taking it up willingly. To begin with, I would remove the record arm as that aria ended; later I found the added balm of sitting through the following gaiety of the full choir chanting, 'His yolk is easy and his burden is light.' Hymns in church mostly seemed hopelessly trite; the beauty of Handel's music and the delight of Schwarzkopf's singing lifted my spirit and filled me with a new dedication to my cause. I was leading a crusade against the baseness which alcohol released in John and I was armed with a determination to vanquish my own baseness and lead him into the new light of truth. I would prick the bubble of his euphoria and enable him to live to see a new dawn, unmarred by delusion. Tolstoy* expressed what I felt when he suggested that to live life and to see only the struggle was like watching an orchestra and seeing only the conductor and players gesticulating, unable to grasp the spiritual ideal, the ennobling splendour of the harmony. I was like a bad amateur player who struggles and sometimes nearly gives up; I knew that I had to keep before me the vision of what life could be, that I must strive to become part of the orchestra and not despair of my own capacity to improve, that just once, perhaps, I might then achieve the ecstacy of becoming part of the whole soaring crescendo of life. I cast John as a horn player with a boil upon his lip who imagines that he can be part of the ensemble without first curing the boil. I had to make it hurt so much that he would cry out for the lesser pain to be endured in its removal but I must not try to suffer the pain for him. I must concentrate on my part of the score whilst he was being cured, so that my performance should not be impaired.

Apart from music, for besides the comfort of *The Messiah* I also found great solace in Mozart whose classical formality met a longing in me for order, I turned to literature. I liked a quotation I read one day from Yeats:

> It seems to me that love, if it is fine, is essentially a discipline. . . . In wise love each divines the high secret self of the other, and refusing to believe in the mere daily self creates a mirror where the lover or the beloved sees an image to copy in daily life.

Idealistic, perhaps, but I determined to create that mirror, to show by my devotion to the good side of John that I believed in him. The great Victorian writers contributed to my visionary notions. They may have been sanctimoniously moral but their

* Tolstoy, *The Kingdom of God is Within You.*

deep perception of human nature was unhindered by the complications of Freudian psychology and I found hope in their books. I disliked the defeatism of the modern novel. I seized upon a paragraph from Trollope:

> He had done wrong, he had sinned grievously; but no sooner did she acknowledge so much than she acknowledged also that a man may sin and yet not be sinful; that glory may be tarnished, and yet not utterly destroyed; that pride may get a fall and yet live to rise again.*

I believed this with all my heart and I longed to transmit my belief to John. I thought that, if I went into his room early in the morning while he was still asleep to wake him with a cup of tea, I must sometime be able to cut through the fog that enveloped his mind before it had time to thicken and infect him with some of my belief and hope. I was persistent and unrelenting in my attempt to pierce his resistance and make him see himself, me, life, in true perspective, and I tried to communicate the love which I felt for him. But one day I found a scrap of paper among his books and read from his handwritten scrawl:

> Words. Sharp razor edged, making little sound, uttered quietly, slipping into the vital parts like a stiletto. Almost silent; perhaps a quiet groan, or rattle pending death. Words. Sharp to catch the wakening worm. Eyes rubbed from sleep, peace; sleep again. No! No! Stiletto words. Cutting, probing consciousness like a scalpel operating upon one small part of the main. Nerves jangle, jangle. Weakest moment. Get. Get. Get him now. Attack! Wretched man defenceless. Don't wait till he's had breakfast under his belt. Food strengthens. Cut him whilst you can.

I gave up then. He did not sense the love, only the reality of pain, and the cruelty of me, the persecutor. For me he could only feel resentment that I interfered in his private life and curbed his freedom. I must detach still further.

I did not know where John obtained the money with which he drank. I never handed him more out of our tight budget than he required for some explicit purpose, and one day I provoked a terrible scene of violence in my anxiety that it should not be dissipated. He had told me that he had none and I handed him

* Anthony Trollope, *The Three Clerks*.

five shillings to buy some small items. He went out to purchase the things and when he came back gave me the change—five shillings and tenpence. I rifled his room and found a letter from an old employee stating that he enclosed five pounds. I was angry that he had taken the money from me when he already had some and told him that I had read the letter. Faced with my illicit knowledge, he shouted at me that he would rather be what he was than a snooper like me. In his anger at my discovery of his double-dealing, he reached down a Japanese sword, acquired in his youth as a souvenir, which I had put, for the children's safety, out of their reach on top of our wardrobe. He faced me in his drunken fury and lifted the sword to my throat. The blade, I knew, still had a fine edge. I stood stolidly and managed not to flinch. As I stared steadily at him, I repeated to myself: 'Though I walk through the valley of the shadow of death, thou shalt not desert me,' and the words gave me courage. For a few agonising seconds, the weapon remained at my neck, then slowly he lowered it, muttering something about the boys. I hid it more effectively after he left the house. It was not only the boys' safety which could be imperilled.

We went away on our holiday, uncertain until the last moment whether John was coming with us. As he was out all through the day before we left, I did not pack his clothes. When he came in, drunk, just as I was finishing, he said:

'Can I help?'

'I've packed our things,' I said. 'If you're coming with us, you'll have to pack your own.'

He came and we secured a short respite. John went to bed each night immediately after dinner. After the first day, he gave me some money which he had had with him; he did not wish to spoil the boys' pleasure. This had always been his practice on holidays in the past but only then did I understand why he had always insisted that I should deal with our holiday finances and why he had always gone to bed so early when we were away. It was his protection against himself in order to spare us.

A month after we came home, John went into hospital, defeated. He had tried to return to his office but had not been wanted. I had sold the car. He had been exposed to his friends. His family no longer gave him the kind of support he wanted. He had no money and nowhere to go. There was nothing to lose.

Chapter Six

ALTHOUGH OUR life together had been strained for many years and the stress of the latter months had been unceasing, I missed John. It was the first time in our sixteen years of married life that he had ever been away from us. I visited the hospital regularly twice a week, once by myself by special bus, and on Sundays when I borrowed my sister's car and took all the children to see their father. He was always glad, at first, to have us with him and I was happy to see that his old easy ability to turn a miserable event into an occasion for laughter was returning. He was undergoing withdrawal treatment and sent to us a cartoon he had sketched of himself laid out on a table, buttocks exposed to a huge, ominous hypodermic syringe poised high above him in the hand of an enormous nurse, whose face was expressive of outrageous enjoyment and anticipation of the impending plunge. He was not confined to the hospital, which was surrounded by vast grounds, and he was fortunate to be in a pleasant new block, cheerfully decorated and curtained, which contrasted favourably with the old Edwardian monstrosity of which it was an extension, whose grim corridors were unsuccessfully relieved by recently hung paintings which only seemed to emphasise the awful bleakness of interminable time stretching before its long-stay patients, its passage hung with film shows and visits from dutiful relatives.

The unit to which John was admitted was not for alcoholics alone; in fact, while he was there, I believe there was only one other. There were drug addicts, and depressives, and neurotics merging into psychotics. At first he slept in a general ward, surrounded by the distressed and distressing groans and cries of people suffering from the hopeless despair of the socially inadequate. Later he was given a room of his own. After two weeks of withdrawal treatment he was seen by the consultant psychiatrist who had visited him at our house, and told that he was to be given aversion treatment. At any time of the day, he would be summoned and given an injection of Apomorphine, a drug which produces violent reaction against alcohol, causing vomiting and headache and unpleasant palpitations. After the injection he would be taken to a room and confronted by an array of bottles and could choose to drink from any he chose. He would take a glass of whisky and immediately be seized by these violent symptoms, retching and incapable of anything but a longing to creep into a hole and die. He could leave the hospital at any time he chose, refusing to suffer such gross maltreatment of his body, but he did not and I admired him for his courage. At first, I had been doubtful of his sincerity. On our second visit, I had seen a raw onion in his locker. He told me that he had had a cold and believed it a good cure, but I knew that he had frequently sought to disguise his breath in the past by eating onions and mistrusted this explanation. I telephoned the hospital after I got home and spoke to the charge nurse, only to be told that the staff could not intervene. If he went out and bought himself a drink, there was nothing to stop him. I was also telephoned by his partner, in those early days, who told me that John had written to him to send him some money; he wanted to buy us all Christmas presents. I hesitated to interfere for if his wish were genuine, it would be unkind to try to stop the money, but I was uneasy. After the treatment began, I felt more confident of John's sincere desire to be cured, for surely he could not submit himself to such degradation without the will for it to succeed.

I had no contact with the psychiatrist at all, and this surprised me, for I had understood from my short contact with the profession that the patient is not now usually regarded as an isolated entity, that all mental illness is related to his background and family. Since the psychiatrist expressed no desire to see me, I determined that I would make an appointment to see him and telephoned his secretary. I was given an appointment for Christmas Eve, and visited him at his office in another hospital. He was a big, impassive man, without humour in his face. He rose upon my entry and, after I was seated, sat himself down behind his desk and leaned back in his chair without speaking. I waited for a few moments but could not out-silence him. There seemed little point in trying. I asked a few questions about John's progress but learnt very little. He told me about the conditioning treatment, of which I already knew. He did not ask me any questions and the meeting was, for me, completely unhelpful. Whether or not he gained any insight from it I do not know.

On Christmas Day, we drove in my sister's car to spend the afternoon with John. I had made a Christmas cake and took this with me, together with some other food, thinking to enrich the hospital fare, but John seemed slightly annoyed by my forethought, having himself been out to buy a small cake. We exchanged presents, and the boys played games but they were fidgety and we were all on edge. We remembered the Christmases of old, when we had had vast family parties and the mood had been genuinely festive, and John relaxed because we were all drinking more than was good for us and he was unexceptional.

As the winter dragged on and then the first signs of spring stirred in the bleak landscape, we began to enjoy our visits. John had lost most of his surplus weight and was looking clear-eyed and healthier than he had for years, and I began to fall in love with him all over again. I felt excitement rise in me as we turned in through the gates of the hospital grounds, and he would come through the swing doors of the ward with a welcome in his face, not only for the boys but also for me, which filled me with happiness. We no longer spent our short two hours in the hospital but drove out into the country and, always, during those Sunday afternoons as we wandered down lanes where the catkins were beginning to drip from the hazel trees, the sun sparkled across the snow-edged fields and seemed to presage a new and happier season in our lives. Michael, David and Andrew, glad in our gladness, ran laughing ahead of us as John and I walked intimately, hand once again in pocketed hand, talking of everything and nothing. James walked more sedately and showed less ebullience than the rest of us but he was tolerant. One day, David brought with him a lifelike toy snake which he laid convincingly on a banking slope and we all shrieked with joy as John tentatively poked it with a stick to see if it was alive. I told John of my progress in sorting out some of the pressing affairs which still beset us when he left home and he no longer resented my attempt to set our economy straight but was glad of what had been done. We spoke hardly at all of his business affairs.

We had already found tenants for the flat before he went into hospital. We disliked having other people in the house, especially since, being nurses, they came in and out at odd hours, but they were pleasant girls and were no trouble. I had always recoiled from the idea of making money out of property and felt absurdly guilty when I collected the rent, even though we provided well-furnished and well-equipped accommodation and could not have survived easily without the income from it. Unfortunately, our first tenants were posted to another hospital six months after they came, and their successors were less thoughtful and considerate, clumping up and down stairs in the heavy wooden shoes which came into fashion at that time, and waking us in the early hours. There was less delicacy, too, in the way they paid their rent and I would cringe inwardly when one of them burst in on us as we sat at a meal, perhaps entertaining the boys' friends, and baldly handed me the money. I was, of course, over-sensitive, and there were many occasions when I had anxiously been awaiting it as it was all that we had to see us through for the following two weeks.

While John was away, I went to see our mortgage company in the north of England. Our mortgage repayments had not been made for many months and we were receiving letters from the building society's solicitors threatening legal action. I had been unaware that we were in arrears because John was responsible for these payments. I had sold the car but this had belonged to his business anyway so that we had received nothing for it ourselves. We were drawing National Health insurance payments for as long as John was in hospital but these would cease when he was discharged and there was no certainty that he would be able to find a job when he came home. His business debts, I learnt from his partner, ran into several thousand pounds and tax was some years in arrear. I had decided that, since I was not responsible for his business affairs, I would not worry about these debts and should certainly not feel any sense of obligation for them, but I had to intervene when it came to maintaining a roof over the heads of the boys and myself. My old friend Joan, with whom I had exchanged grumbles before I understood the root of our troubles, had moved to the north, and I invited myself to visit her for a few days while my parents came back to look after the boys. I was touched, before I went, to receive a first-class return train ticket and sufficient money to buy myself a good meal on the train, from my father, who was himself by this time a pensioner, and I basked in the comfort of unaccustomed privilege as I travelled northwards. Joan met me at the station and took me home with her to be cossetted and strengthened with loving care.

One day in her company was a tonic. She is a person who always draws the love and affection of her friends through the generosity of her personality. She lost her husband because of her loving nature; he was unable to tolerate the way she gave so much of herself to those in trouble, demanding her sole attention, jealous of her undemanding love of other people, and they were divorced. When we talked, we realised that Joan and her husband had stayed together for years because they considered that separation might be harmful to their two children in their formative years, whereas I knew that I would only leave John if I felt that his continuing presence might be harmful to the children. For Joan, the maternal instinct was the strongest and she mothered everybody; for me, the pairing instinct prevailed and I found it difficult to mother anybody. She, I felt, was a much nicer person. She mothered me and I relaxed.

In my bitterest moments, I had frequently accused John of wanting not a wife but a mother. When he is ill, I become intolerable because I am constantly aware of his longing to be nursed with devoted attention; when I become sexually desperate, John is evasive or seeks to satisfy me with mechanical lovemaking that drives me to despair; he does not feel the intense involvement in the moment to the exclusion of any other awareness. 'You know that bus-stop on the left side of the bridge . . .' he says, as I am about to drown in sensual ecstasy.

Joan and I discussed whether I should visit the building society dressed sombrely, with a haggard face devoid of make-up, that would arouse compassionate pity for my distressed plight, or whether I should tart myself up and impress them with my brave fortitude in the face of impending disaster, which only they could cause to be averted. On consideration, I naturally preferred the courageous front. In the event, I doubt whether it made any difference. The society was helpful, listened understandingly to my explanation that my husband had suffered a mental breakdown, and agreed with my suggestions for renewing the payments. I had cast them in the role of wicked landlord about to evict the innocent mother and children into the streets and found, instead, an inoffensive, clerkish representative glad to be relieved of the need to distrain upon our property.

On my journey home, I again gloried in the corner seat of a first-class carriage with only one other occupant. I had planned to study, for I was in the second year of my diploma course and my examination was imminent, but instead I fell into conversation with my companion. It was pleasant to range over the subjects which interested me and find that he responded with evident enjoyment for, when the steward came along the corridor asking if we were dining and I shook my head, he asked me to join him. I had not dined alone with another man since I had been married and I felt boosted by this encounter. It made me realise that I had not lost all my feminine attractiveness.

My friends and family, too, helped me to maintain hope and courage for they gave me the impression that they respected me for my refusal to be defeated and I believe that my early decision to accept our circumstances without bitterness or recrimination was one which helped me when I needed to draw on their goodwill. There may have been a certain reservation in their view of me, a recoiling from the tough attitude which refused to allow John the comfort of sympathy and, to those I cared about, I tried to explain the need for him to rely upon himself which would be undermined if I were soft with him. I thought they understood, until one day, shortly before John came home, when Kenneth Wilson was driving me home from a meeting we had both attended at the boys' school, he stopped the car and said: 'You know, don't you, Mary, that it's going to be difficult for John when he comes home.'

'Yes,' I said.

'We realise that you cannot feel the same way about him that you used to, but he is going to need affection.'

'But, Ken,' I said. 'I love him. Don't you know I've fallen in love with him all over again; I get just as excited when I see him now as I did when we were engaged.'

'Oh,' he said, relieved and slightly embarrassed. 'No, I didn't realise. Oh well, then, I don't need to say any more.'

'No.'

He started the car with the air of a man saved the unpleasant task of delivering a difficult but necessary homily. He was kind, for he was concerned for both of us.

Perhaps he had been misled by my behaviour a few weeks earlier, when he had helped me to dismantle John's local office which had been fitted and furnished with reckless disregard for expense. There was some good new carpeting laid up the stairs and in all the rooms, and I wished to lift this and get it transported home where we were sadly in need of new carpeting.

There were so many holes in the floor covering in the living-room that anyone entering it was in danger of tripping and falling headlong over the bare threads. I had obtained permission from John's partner to remove it and to clear the furniture. Kenneth volunteered to come along and do the more strenuous tasks of shifting furniture and pulling up the carpet tacks. As we cleared the rooms and I went through the cupboards, I became light-headed from the sight of their contents. There were numerous empty shirt-boxes; I think John must have gone out and bought a new shirt at least once a week: did it make him feel more respectable? Tucked away in corners were the inevitable, ubiquitous empty bottles. Towards the end of our task, tired and grimy, I took one out and held it up to the light.

'God,' I said. 'He might have left a little in just one of them.'

My final action was to unscrew the notice outside the main door which announced the business. I felt no regret for the shattered dreams of ambition and success that this dismantling represented, only a huge sense of relief that yet another meglomanic delusion was being swept away. To Ken, it must have seemed sad to participate in the destruction of a man's enterprise. I looked neither back nor forward and channelled all my initiative and energy into making our present condition of living tenable. Every extravagance or unnecessary expense had to be eliminated if we were to maintain ourselves without further descent into poverty, and sentimental longings for what might have been were outlawed from my mind.

The consultant psychiatrist summoned me to his office a week before John's discharge. Again his impassive urbanity and lack of response to my desire for a clear opinion of the chances of the success of his treatment left me feeling thwarted and unsure. He would make no prognosis. He asked whether I wanted John home.

'Oh, yes,' I said. 'I've missed him. He really is a very nice person, isn't he?'

He grunted noncommittally, and I disliked him for refusing to reinforce my judgement.

He told me that, when John was discharged, he would be given Antibuse tablets which he would have to take each morning. If he drank after one of those, he would suffer very unpleasant physical reactions.

'Keep him in the habit of taking one at breakfast time,' he said.

'Do you mean that I have to take the responsibility of keeping him sober?'

'To begin with, he may find it difficult.'

'You mean he may still want to drink after all this aversion treatment?'

'He may.'

'So that, for the rest of our lives, I may have to take the burden?'

'Yes. Do you think you can carry it?'

'I suppose so,' I said. I was disappointed. I had thought John was supposed to be cured.

The first month after his homecoming was, for me, and for the boys, happier than our lives had been for years. John co-operated in the house and took over some of the drudgery of domestic work. He went to sign up at the local Labour Exchange and put himself on the books of the Executive and Professional Registry. It was early spring, and he worked hard in the garden while I was able to spend more time working at my books as my examination approached. They were halcyon days, without moodiness or intemperance. He had lost all the heavy coarseness which so repulsed me and looked twenty years younger than he had only three months earlier. I wrote a joyous letter to Joan, and she replied that it read like a letter from a newly-wed. I did have the realism to add, at the end, that the enchanted bubble would, I knew, burst once it felt the pressure of economic necessity and John's obligation to accept some responsibility, but I felt that we both needed this period of domestic quietude even though we were now living on weekly payments from the social security department to augment our small rent income. I allowed myself to wait until I had sat my examination.

Once my self-determined time limit was reached, I started to wonder whether John was really seriously looking for a job. He did not appear to be doing so with much enthusiasm. I began to make suggestions and the easy atmosphere which we had enjoyed deteriorated. I liked lounging in a deckchair in the afternoon sun, talking idly with John, but I did not like the sense I had of time running out. I had arranged with the building society that our repayments would begin once again in June and we would certainly not be able to afford them on our present income. I did not feel too inferior at the thought of living off the State for a short while, but I was not happy to prolong the parasitism of our existence. A kind sister had presented me with a cheque for one hundred pounds which enabled me to buy the boys some badly needed clothes and I was grateful for her generosity, but I knew that we were living on the accumulation of past acquisitions that I would not be able to replace as these wore out. I had long since sold my diamong ring. I had little sense of pride debarring me from accepting acts of charity to tide us over our period of crisis, but I was not prepared to undergo a lengthy beggarliness. As John became aware of my sense of frustration that he did nothing to relieve the situation, hostility crept back into our relationship. He continued to take his Antibuse tablets but, twice, he retired to bed his face diffused, his eyes popping, complaining of a severe headache. My suggestion that he had taken a drink was denied, but I knew that I was witnessing the symptoms described to me by the psychiatrist. One day, our G.P. called on me while John was out and expressed anxiety about the tablets. He said that they could produce fatal results if John drank. He also said that if John remained dry for several years, there might come a time when he would be able to drink socially in a normal way. I urgently requested him not to make this suggestion to John, who would welcome any encouragement.

I continued to remind him to take his tablets but not with any sense that they established a secure base for sobriety. The knowledge that he had been dosed for that day simply eased my mind. If I tried to talk to John about his attitudes and feelings, he retired into silence. He was not prepared to volunteer any information about what he was thinking. When, one day, I reached down the bottle of Antibuse and looked at the tablet which I shook out to hand to him, I realised with a shock that it was codeine, which is marked by a one-line indentation; Antibuse, which is the same size and colour, has a crossed-line indentation. I felt utterly defeated and expressed my contempt at this trick. Despite the cessation of the daily dose, which I now felt to be gratuitous, John did not appear to drink much. The very fact that he drank at all made me realise that, if he did find a job, the chances were that we should soon find that his alcohol consumption went up as soon as he had money in his pocket. I began to see his period in hospital as an experiment in behaviourist psychology, suited to rats or pigeons without the intelligence to reason out the cause of the physical distress brought about by the consumption of alcohol; for a period I had allowed my mind the lie quiescent under the sedative of an unintelligent subservience to professional expertise. But I had been disappointed that there appeared to have been no attempt at probing analysis of John's personality or encouragement for him to seek in himself the cause of his addiction.

He painted a little and seemed happy when he was absorbed in this pastime. I wondered whether he had really been working in a profession which was not suited to his nature. I was well aware that domesticity was not my forté and could see no valid reason why, if John preferred it, we should not exchange roles. Tentatively one morning in June, I suggested to him that perhaps he was more suited than I to the home environment. I did not wish to undermine his manhood and I built up a picture of the self-fulfilling life he could lead, developing his talent for painting and possibly selling his pictures, while I went out to work. He agreed that we should try this arrangement and I began to seek a job which I, too, would find congenial. I had none but secretarial qualifications and confidence in my own ability to work intelligently and I was determined to find employment which would interest me. After looking around locally, I realised that if I wanted something both remunerative and absorbing, I should have to work in London where the variety of possible choices was wide. To tide us over the next few weeks and to save the cost of fares from home without compensatory income, I worked as a temporary shorthand-typist in a pleasant, but dull, office near the terminus, and was allowed unpaid time off to go to interviews. After six weeks, I had learnt not to be completely frank. I realised that prospective employers were going to want to know how I proposed to work full-time with four children and not expect to have to be absent when they were unwell. If I were to obtain a job with any responsibility, I had to convince them of my complete reliability. At first, I told them that my husband was a recovered alcoholic, that he would be at home to care for the children and there would be no problem at all. I found interest, curiosity and sympathy, but a lack of conviction that they would be able to rely on me. If the job was unresponsible and, therefore, in my view, uninteresting, the employer was willing to take the risk. If the job, for me, was desirable, I was told: 'We'd like to have you, but . . .' So when I finally attended an interview for a job involved with keeping an educational department running smoothly administratively as well as performing secretarial duties, where I should not be personal handmaiden and, as the advertisements so succinctly put it, Girl Friday to one man, my own personality trimmed and tapered to meet his requirements, subservient to his needs and protector of his egotism, I decided to gloss over the true story. After a lifetime of endeavouring to satisfy my husband and adapt myself to his requirements, with lamentable lack of success, I had no wish to place myself in the position of dogsbody to another man. When the personnel officer asked me how I proposed to work and cope with my family, I explained that my husband was a talented painter who longed to have the time to develop his art; that he had suffered a minor breakdown in his attempt to confine himself in a niche that did not fit him, and that we had both decided, since I was undomesticated, that a reversal of roles would suit us admirably. The kind man listened to me with interest and found me credible. He even allowed himself a moment of self-indulgent fantasy as he pictured how well such an arrangement might suit him, too, if his wife would only co-operate. He told me that the job I was seeking required great tact, because I would be dealing with a variety of intellectuals who each considered his own work had a priority over anybody else's, that I would have to keep the machine in my small section running smoothly and that I would be the only person who would know what was going on all the time, that the office had been rather badly mismanaged for a considerable period and that it needed a firm new hand to put it into order, and that I would have an assistant to help me. He was a marvellous personnel officer. He charmed me into believing that he had been waiting for me to turn up for years, and convinced me of my ability to manoeuvre all those scholastic, unpractical children (for so, I felt, he regarded these men of letters) into docility. The pay was rather less than I should have received in a commercial enterprise. I was offered the job and I accepted his proffered challenge with enthusiasm. I worked in the department for two years and found it a haven of involvement and interest which enabled me to face a steadily declining situation at home. I was never bored and had no time to brood unhappily over John's deterioration during the hours I was at my office. I met a large number of interesting, intelligent people from all over the world, and I was very conscious that I had carved out a place for myself in an environment which pleased me and in which I was appreciated. When I left it, I felt a wrench and had the gratifying sensation of knowing that I would be missed—for a short while. I was reticent about my home life and, therefore, if at times I appeared obviously under strain, nobody asked questions and I was not tempted to seek their sympathy. This separation of my home and office lives was essential for my stability. I tried not to let the exhaustion I sometimes felt affect the quality of my work and certainly did not let it interfere with my apparent emotional equilibrium. From this sanctuary of mutual goodwill, at least between me and my academic and administrative colleagues—there was plenty of in-fighting between them which I watched with non-partisan interest—I returned home refreshed.

At first, the arrangement appeared to be working. John coped with the boys, did the shopping, kept the house clean and even cooked the evening meal. Understandably, he did not find a lot of time for painting. I knew myself the discipline needed to make time in a housewife's day for personal interests. He had little contact with other people. He started to attend a morning painting class, but gave that up after three sessions—I doubt that he felt at home among the middle-aged women who made up most of the class, but I was sorry that he did not persevere. Within a few weeks, he began drinking in earnest again. One evening, when I arrived home, I was met by the simpering, unfocused smile compounded of the awareness of his guilt and apprehension of my reaction, covered by an attempt to hide both beneath a false affability. He denied that he was drunk, of course. I decided that I should have to do all the shopping myself rather than hand over to him any part of our limited income. It put an extra toll on me but this was better than seeing the housekeeping money swallowed up by the provision of booze for John. Throughout the winter, I was never sure what I should come home to. Sometimes all was well, James and Michael buckling down to their homework, the little boys laughing and splashing in their bath with John telling them the stories which he was so good at inventing; at others, as I opened the front door, I knew from the unnatural quiet that the children were all in their rooms trying to apply themselves to occupations that would not incur their father's irritation or wrath. The days on which

Michael bicycled down to the station to meet me were the days on which I knew that John was at his worst, and as we walked up the road, Michael would tell me how, immediately he arrived home from school, he had been told to get the tea, or run down to the shops to buy some cake. I hated to think that they, too, were coming home to uncertainty and resented the fact that John expected the children, after their day's work, to do the tasks which he was at home all day to do, but there was little I could do. David, now nearly eight, the happy, uncomplicated child who liked everybody around him to be happy too, became hurt and bewildered by John's unfair outbursts against James and Michael. We tried to explain to him that he must try to find what pleasure he could in his own occupations and not become involved in other people's dissensions, but it was difficult for him to accept the need to become detached when his father was moody and unhappy, for he loved John dearly and his sensitive heart sensed when he was in pain. I was confident that John would not seek to hurt him or Andrew intentionally, as he did myself and his elder brothers, and David, too, was conscious that when they were alone together the atmosphere was less fraught with underlying tensions. During the Easter holidays, I sent James and Michael away to stay with friends and, because he had the small boys alone with him all day, John sought to entertain them and keep them happy and restrained his need to drink. But, one day, when I arrived home, I found that they had all been to the swimming-baths with one of John's old drinking friends and he was over cheerful. As I came in, his face changed from inebriated goodwill to the hard hostility with which he countered my comprehending look. I had learnt to slip on a mask of detachment the moment I had assessed the situation and he must have hated this; perhaps he read more disdain in it that I intended. Certainly, if I had not been there, any onlooker would have thought what a cheerful, noisy threesome they were. David, wise beyond his years, agreed vehemently with me when I said I thought I should not have the evening meal with them.

'Yes, Mummy,' he said. 'It would be better if you went out.'

So I took myself off to Diana and Bill up the road in order that David and Andrew should not have to witness the inevitable vilification that I would undergo if I remained, and could go to bed undisturbed by a change in their father's mood and a tense brightness in mine. If I had been able to overcome my refusal, just occasionally, to allow John to feel that despite the alcohol in him I could still show affection, it may have been easier for the boys, but I had set myself upon a course of emotional disengagement and I could not vacillate in my reaction to his drinking without fear of losing my equilibrium.

Throughout the following summer, I became more and more concerned for the boys. I do not know where John obtained the money to enable him to drink but his consumption was steadily increasing. I did not fear that he would harm them physically, but the emotional strain to which they were subjected frightened me, and I began, also, to wonder whether it was safe to allow them to be in his care. He met the little ones from school and I imagined them knocked down through a misjudged crossing of the main road in heavy traffic. Andrew who, unlike David, never outwardly expressed any feeling of concern, began to grow paler and paler, and was often a taut little figure in his bed, his face white against the pillow, when I went to kiss him goodnight.

'Is anything worrying you, Andrew?'

'No,' he would say, and his mouth would shut firmly.

David would tell me that, to-day, Daddy had been unkind to Michael, sweeping his model soldiers off the table so that some of them broke.

'But don't tell him I told you,' he would plead. 'It will only make him cross.'

I was racked by uncertainty. I knew that we could not continue to live in this way for much longer but was loathe to give up my job. If I stayed at home all the time, with John steadily declining both mentally and physically, it would surely begin to reflect upon my own stability. At least, with the children, I was usually able to maintain an outward balance now and I tried not to project on to them my own anxiety. I hated the thought of returning to a state of dependence on national assistance and yet, was I, by my daily withdrawal from the scene, laying upon the boys a burden which I should carry myself? I began to contemplate separation from John, and told him that, unless things improved, I might have to leave him.

'I don't care a damn if you go,' he said. 'You are the cause of all the unhappiness in this house. But you won't get the children. I shall fight you through the courts and you won't stand a chance.'

I reserved my own judgement on that, and did not argue.

Living became pain. Whilst I was at my office, I cut off from my problems, and whilst I was at home I tried to deal with each crisis as it arose, and fell into bed too tired not to sleep, but the periods between, the walk from the office to station, the train journey, and the walk home, when I had time to think, hurt. I could see no end to this everlasting conflict and as I sought, round and round in my mind, for some clear definition of purpose, for the goal I was trying to reach beyond the tensions of each day, I longed to lean on somebody else, to lay down the load and relax. I thought I had stopped trying to control John but I could not let go of the responsibility which rested on me to try to prevent his actions from controlling all of us. The only way I could do that was to leave him, and I was not really ready to throw in my hand and say: 'Destiny, you've won.' I wanted to remain his wife, and I could not let go of my vision of a united family. I am glad now that I held on to that vision.

I did have faith in the ultimate victory of good over evil and I knew that if I succumbed to despair I would open a huge fissure through which only worse evil, in the shape of my own disintegration, would be able to flood. I clung to the certainty that John's natural kindness and love for us all was perverted only by his inability to face life and himself without the relief that drink afforded him by obscuring the hard, unrelenting details, and that the awareness of his dependence which we had forced upon him made him hate us for reminding him of his weakness. Without the controlling influence of a mind capable of rational acceptance of his own responsibility, he could only lash out at us in an attempt to escape his burden of guilt and hopelessness.

So, nightly, I braced myself to face what might be and not allow the boys to feel the extent of my effort. Sometimes, of course, I slipped badly. One evening when I arrived home, John was out and the boys fearful of his return. I sat down at the kitchen table and gave way to my own apprehension. I could not stand another brazen attempt to put me in the wrong; I knew that I should scream with frustration at his refusal to acknowledge his own culpability. I laid my head upon the table and wept, the boys standing around impotent in their desire to help.

'Get Diana,' I sobbed.

Michael ran out to fetch her, and she came running back with him.

She put her arm around my shoulders and gently led me back to her own house. I heard Michael say:

'Don't worry about us. We can manage.'

I leaned against the warmth of Diana and told her of my fear; how night after night I had to guard myself against losing control and how, tonight, I could not face John's return. She fed me tea and gently assured me of her love and understanding. Bill came in as I released the tension within me in a torrent of sobbing and let the tiredness overwhelm me in the unwonted comfort of quiet sympathy. And it was he who gave me the strength to return and the will to fight on, through his own normality.

As he made to sit down in an armchair, Diana said:

'Weren't you going to help Bobby with his homework, darling?'

'He's finished,' said Bill, as he eased himself back.

Through my self-pity, I felt a surge of laughter well up in me. Whether Bill was unaware of the hint in his wife's remark I do not know, but if he was he chose to ignore it. He wasn't going to have his evening disturbed by an hysterical woman. I sat up and blew my nose and inwardly thanked Bill for his imperturbability. Life went on all around me and there was no reason why I should not take and enjoy my share of it. There was sense in continuing to strive because people like Bill could be unconfounded by tragedy, and tragedy so quickly became comic. I went back home and the boys were manifestly thankful to learn that Mum had recovered and was even capable of cooking their dinner.

Then, in June, AA came back into our lives, in the shape of an ebullient, vociferous, outrageous man named Guy. How he was drawn in, I do not know. I had not sought help again. John knew where he could go if he wanted to find understanding but I had long since accepted that he had to go of his own volition. I no longer had contact with Al-Anon for there was no group nearby and I lacked the time to travel to a distant meeting. I felt that I had got its essential message of my inability to stop John drinking if he did not want to and the need to concentrate on my own survival. Perhaps John himself telephoned in a moment of desperation, but he has no recollection of doing so. I only knew the relief, after I had arrived home one evening to find him dabbing splodges of paint at and ruining one of his own pictures with the unfocused determination of complete intoxication, when the front doorbell rang and I opened it to a large stranger.

'I'm Guy,' he said. 'I've come to take John to an AA meeting.'

'Thank goodness,' I said.

I took him in to John and he immediately saw how drunk he was.

'I don't think it will do him much good tonight,' said Guy.

'I don't care whether it does him any good or not,' I said. 'Just take him away for a little while.'

He followed me into the kitchen where the boys were messing around, waiting for me to prepare their evening meal.

'He'll have to go into hospital,' said Guy.

I was disturbed that he spoke so baldly before the children. I would have preferred that they should have had the fragmentation of all our hopes that he would himself be able to find the will to live without the aid of alcohol less bluntly stated.

'Maybe,' I said, 'but please take him away now.' I only just prevented myself from physically pushing them both out of the front door.

Guy persevered and bludgeoned his way into John's resistant consciousness as our previous AA contact had lacked the personality to do. He maintained telephone contact with John over several months and frequently arrived at the house unheralded. He took him to meetings and introduced another AA member who lived nearby, a woman called Sylvia who had maintained her sobriety for long enough to be a safe sponsor, to drive him to distant meetings that Guy himself was unable or disinclined to attend. These meetings appeared to have little effect on John's drinking, but the constant association with people who had sunk to the same or much worse depths of degradation than he himself and were now leading positive, constructive lives must have begun to erode his own belief that he was unique, that he was a case beyond redemption and that any effort on his own part was pointless because it must only lead to failure. AA meetings are not designed as an evening's occupation for the alcoholic, to relieve his family of his onerous presence, but we found great release in the knowledge that John's absence did not simply mean that his later return would inflict yet worse tensions upon us. He was picked up and delivered home to us and we knew that he would be sober, or at least less drunk, and we were able to recover a little from the stresses of uncertainty.

I think Guy's companionship was healthy for John. Guy was extrovert and, though he never relaxed in his attempt to make John face his disability and admit it, he also made us all laugh with his extravagant stories of his own past. He introduced into our situation an element of humour, and John had always been more open to suggestions of ludicrousness than to solemn exhortation. I found Guy exhausting with his unceasing flow of self-castigation intermixed with improbable anecdotes and I doubted his complete authenticity. I knew that he verbally flagellated himself in order to encourage John to acknowledge his own faults, and I now almost believe his stories. He has a remarkably perceptive eye and can extract from any situation an excess of enjoyment which to me is immoderate but I know now my own inability to live easily and with unequivocal delight in the stupidity of our human race. Guy loves his fellow men though he disguises this with a flamboyant display of aggression and an intractable refusal to allow them to deceive themselves in their foolish attempts to justify their deficiencies. The kindness in him shines through his blunt manner.

One day, I heard him say to John:

'You will have to go to hospital, you know. You could get into the alcoholic unit at Benstead.'

'But Mary would not be able to manage,' said John, bleakly.

'Yes, I would,' I called, from the kitchen. 'I'm sure we could easily arrange something.'

Although John was frequently drunk in the evening, he still did a fair amount of housekeeping in the day-time and I did not have to clean the house or make the beds or wash up the breakfast dishes. He was also at home if any of the children was sick, and, usually, when they came home from school, though the latter was a dubious asset.

The thought of the necessity of undergoing yet more treatment must have nagged at him, for he became even more unpredictable. For days he was conscientious in fulfilling the role he had agreed to take on and we would relax. Then, once again, the demon of drink would grip him.

Even Guy finally said: 'He is not ready yet. He has not reached his rock bottom. You're still propping him up too much.'

'I know,' I said, 'but I must. We're in the process of selling the house and until that's organised, I cannot manage alone. He is being sensible about this and he seems anxious that we should not suffer materially any more. He wants to make sure that we're safe from his being able to cause us any more harm. I know that.'

Our house was in an area that was gradually being demolished.

In the past, we had had several tempting offers for it from firms who wanted to develop the site, but I had always resisted them. I loved my home. I disliked the idea of selling it and profiteering—to me an ugly word, reeking of shameful self-aggrandisement. But now, with our whole environment changing and new flats erected all around us, with neighbours willing to sell, and the knowledge of John's huge business overdraft and debts which could be partly paid off out of our profit, it seemed foolish to be restrained by sentiment or idealistic principles. I realised that I must put the boys and myself first. It would be a false sort of idealism to allow John to be made bankrupt, as seemed probable, and the inevitable deterioration in our life style which would follow, because of my convictions. I had agreed to sell the house and we had begun to look at other properties. I had little time, and we had no transport. With the aid of my sister's car, we looked at three houses, all much smaller than our present one, on three consecutive week-ends. We contracted to buy the third. I saw it twice and signed the contract. John insisted that it should be in my name. He never swerved in his determination to make sure that we were as secure as possible whatever befell him, and I clung to this knowledge of him when he was at his drunken worst. It made it clear that his actions did not entirely represent his deepest feelings for us. It was four months before we were able to move, for our vendors were having a bungalow built for them and it would not be ready until the following February, and I did not see the house again until the week before we moved in. By then, I could scarcely remember what it was like.

In the meantime, Guy had given up too. He retired, grumbling that he did not accept defeat easily and looking accusingly at me because I could not bring myself to take the final step which would leave John entirely isolated. He realised my need to hang on until we had made the move, for I had little time to deal with the complexities of the transfer of our household and John, in anything related to the negotiations for the sale of our present house, was clear-minded and efficient. Sylvia still picked him up once a week to take him to a meeting, and she too told me that I was propping John. Occasionally, he even took himself spontaneously to another meeting. One night, while James and I were relaxing in the sitting-room, trying to muster the energy to take ourselves to bed, he came back with a companion. He was a man whom he said he had met at the meeting, and whom I had seen occasionally serving customers from a fruit and vegetable stall which I sometimes used in the High Street. When this man was there, I avoided it for he revolted me. He looked dirty and scabrous and I did not want to buy anything which he had touched. I was furious that John had brought such a distasteful character into our home and recoiled from the thought of his contaminating our furniture. James, too, was outraged, for he is a fastidious boy. When John told me that he was going to put the man to bed in our spare room, I felt sick. With a determination to help this poor fellow sufferer and allow him to feel, for one night, the comfort of a home, he ignored our unconcealed aversion and went upstairs to run the bath. James went to bed and left me with my unwelcome guest. Lacking a fragment of that strange, unusual compassion that stirred in Sally Trench when she went out nightly to succour the meths drinkers of London, I kept my distance. The man scarcely comprehended where he was but he must have sensed the loathing I felt for him. Mixed with the distaste, though, was a tinge of shame that I could not feel any pity, that I could only think of myself and my own feelings. John took him to the bathroom and undressed him, scrubbed him and put him to bed. I retired myself, refusing to have anything to do with the affair. I could not bring myself to insist that he must go—and I doubt that John would have taken any notice of me if I had—so I preferred to remain aloof. In the morning, when I got up, the man had gone, roused and fed by John who, accepting my prudish behaviour without comment, was by then poking the sheets in which he had slept into the washing-machine. I cannot forget my lack of charity. I have heard since that the man is dead, burnt in a fire which he himselt probably caused in a dilapidated property where he sought shelter for the night. With the memory is the knowledge that I have changed very little, that I would still want to turn away, like the priest and the Levite, from my neighbour if I did not recognise myself in him. I could not identify with that man and therefore I could not love him.

Chapter Seven

It was a different sort of detachment which enabled me to withstand John's subtler attacks upon my forbearance. One night, he came in late to find the supper dishes unwashed upon the draining-board. I had left them while I completed some mending of the children's clothes, planning to tackle them before I went to bed. John did not come in to me and accuse me of sluttish neglect as he once would have done. He went upstairs and pulled a sleeping James out of bed, pushed him downstairs and told him that he was lazy, that he did not help his mother as he should, and to get on now and get the kitchen clear. Poor James, dazed, stood at the sink and looked helplessly at me for succour. I managed to ignore the plea. I knew that John was trying to upset me by using James as his whipping boy but I knew, also, that I must not react; if it did not work this time, the likelihood of this ploy being repeated was less. The strain of the necessity for constant suppression of my instincts and emotions took its toll. One Sunday evening, when the children were noisy, the house in disarray from the week-end, John unco-operative, and with the thought of having to return to work the next day and the next and the next with no time to organise any order into our daily living and the responsibility heavy upon me, I could no longer bear it. I burst out against them all, not only John. Half-way through trying to yank a reluctant Andrew out of the bath, I broke.

'I'm sick of you all,' I shouted. 'I'm tired of having to do everything. If you want to live in squalor, you can. You none of you ever clear up your mess. You think, because I'm here, I shall do it for you. Well, I'm not going to. I'm going out.'

I went downstairs, called the dog, and left the house.

I walked through the suburban streets, my eyes on the ground, unconscious of my surroundings, uncaring for how the boys would feel, unaware of where my steps were taking me. As I walked, I longed for somebody to rest my head against, for a recognition of my yearning to share my endless problems. If Ken, reliable Ken, should drive past me now and stop, and open the car door, I wondered if I would get in and turn to him for comfort, whether if he indicated any feeling for me I would respond, forgetting my loyalty, releasing all my suppressed sexuality and seeking to replenish my emotional bankruptcy out of the tenderness of another man's love. I allowed my imagination to roam.

I found myself in a large deserted park. It was evening and the day had been wet so that there were none of the Sunday, ball-pitching children there shouting as their fathers, shirts open at office-white necks, played with them in obligatory family enjoyment, mothers in stockinged feet padding after the ball thrown wide, indulgent grandmothers seated on the ground with the tea picnic hamper beside them; there were no dogs scampering around, sniffing and wagging their tails in the weekly circumscribed abandon of the family outing. There was no-one there, and the grass was wet and I felt a primordial urge to become part of the earth, to submerge myself in the trees and the sky. I took off my sandals and walked, barefooted, finding delight in the touch of the damp ground as it oozed up between my toes. I walked across the undemanding spaciousness and felt again joy returning to me, the joy of being alive. I came out through woods upon a road which trailed past tiny smallholdings towards the Downs; calling the dog to me, I slipped my feet back into my sandals and we walked along, countrywise on the right side of the road, as the Sunday evening traffic flowed past us. On the Downs, there were wild scabious and hardheads fresh waving in the tardy dying pale sunshine of a wet summer's day. I danced upon the deserted Downs and sang all the exultant songs I could recall. I picked a bouquet of wild flowers and revelled in an involuntary banishment of thought which made me slightly mad.

I reached home three hours after I had left to find the house tidied and the boys subdued and concerned for my well-being. David was in bed but still awake, anxious.

'I was worried about you,' he said.

'I'm sorry, darling. I'm all right now. I went for a long walk with Buster and feel much better. Go to sleep, now.'

When I came downstairs, John was preparing supper and the evening was placid.

During that summer, James and Michael went away again. My mother invited the two small boys to spend a few days with her. I had been able to face returning from work when the children were there but, with them away, I knew that I must have some relief from the uncertainty of my reception from John. Without the boys to consider, I knew that the chances of his remaining sober all day were slender. One of my sisters came to fetch the little boys for their visit and I asked her whether I might stay with her during their absence. So, for the first time, we all left him.

When I returned from work three days later, he made no show of welcome. Defiant, he had not hidden the bottles but left them empty and obvious outside the kitchen door. Later, one of our tenants brought down some records which she said John had left in the flat and, when I was going through his drawers, as I frequently did in order to see whether he had any money, I found a small silver cross on a chain. I wondered where it came from. He had apparently sought the company of the girls upstairs and it crossed my mind that he may even have sought more than friendly companionship. When, two days later, one of them came down and told me that they wished to give notice and leave in two weeks, the thought flitted through my head that perhaps she considered it improper for them to remain. Her friend was a rather lonely, isolated girl without boy-friends of her own. I pushed away further unprofitable conjecture. I had deserted John and, if he had sought comfort elsewhere, I could scarcely complain. It was only later, as one crowded journey home I felt the knee of a standing women press hard against mine in the packed compartment, that the picture of two bodies straining against one another leapt with desperate clarity into my mind. I concentrated on the book I was reading.

Perhaps because he was involved in positive activity in the sale of our house, which would mitigate a little our increasing poverty and would make less likely his being made bankrupt, John rallied himself that September. For nearly two weeks I arrived home to find dinner prepared, the boys in high spirits and John pleasant and friendly. Homecoming became a pleasure. Then, the night before James's birthday, as I opened the front door I felt the ominous quietness in the house. I walked into the dining-room and David was on the floor playing with a car; he glanced towards the kitchen where John was standing over the cooker. I went in and said 'Hallo', and John said 'Hallo', and I knew he had been drinking. I did not kiss him as had been my recent custom. As I went upstairs to take off my coat, he followed me, anxious to tell me that he had remembered to prepare for James's birthday. He took me to his bedroom and said he had sent Michael down to the shops to buy James's present, despite the fact that he had himself been out twice.

'Oh dear, you've been drinking to-day,' I said.

'Don't be ridiculous,' he countered, and went away.

I went into Michael's room and raised my eyebrows questioningly. Michael nodded his head, and told me that he had come home at lunch-time to find the door open and John out. He had made himself some lunch and John had come back and tried to talk to him about poetry in the rambling, tedious way he had when his mind was fuddled with alcohol. James was on his bed reading.

I returned downstairs to the kitchen and John said, sarcastically: 'It's always such a pleasure to have you home.'

We had dinner and the boys and I talked. John left the table with his plate saying he preferred to eat elsewhere. We all felt relief and were able to relax without his brooding presence at the head of the table. After dinner, I went upstairs to his room and felt in his pockets. I had given him three pounds that morning to shop for James's birthday. I found one pound and stuffed it under the pillow of my bed. After I had put the little boys to bed, Michael and I decided to take the dog for a walk. John was washing up. On these occasions when he had reverted to drinking, he would often attempt to keep up the pretence that he was sober, doing routine jobs perhaps in an endeavour to convince us that our conclusions were unfounded: he frequently left the job, though, half completed.

I called from the hall: 'Michael and I are going out.'

'Oh, no, you're not,' came his threatening reply.

We skipped quickly out of the front door and were away down the road. I did not think he would bother to follow us.

When we got back, John came out of the sitting-room and said:

'I want a word with you.'

He pointed upstairs and I went ahead of him to my bedroom. He shut the door and said: 'Where is the pound note you stole?'

'It was my change,' I said. 'The boys are going to the cinema for James's birthday and I need it to give to them.'

'I shall hit you if you don't give it to me,' John's voice was low, but ominous.

I braced myself and stood still, and he saw that I was going to let him hit me without attempting to protect myself.

He threatened again, and I stood facing him, looking straight into his eyes. He hit me across the face, twice.

'Mary, I don't want to do this but you are making me,' he said.

I said nothing.

'If you don't give me that pound I will make you.'

He threw me on to the bed. He began to look in my bag and then changed his mind because tonight he had decided that I was a thief and he must not lower himself to my level. I had to give him back the money and so admit my guilt. He hit me again instead. He seized me by the throat and raised his clenched hand again in fury. I lay inert upon the bed and looked unswervingly at him. He hit me once or twice more, pummelling my body, and then sat down beside me and said that he would stay there until I told him where the money was. I took off my shoes. As he heaved the mattress, with me on top of it, off the bed, in thwarted fury at his inability to intimidate me, the bookcase went over but I caught the lamp as it went and saved it from crashing. I landed on the floor in a tumble of bedclothes and he seized the base of the bed and tipped that over so that I was penned into my corner.

'I will smash up this room if you don't tell me where that pound is,' he threatened.

I sat still.

He began to heave over the weighty chest-of-drawers in which I stored blankets and the children's clothes. All the drawers slid out and one fell on his leg. The jars and bottles which had been on top scattered in a welter of confusion across the carpet. He menaced me again and seeing me immobile and apparently insensate, turned and smashed his fist down upon the glass which lay across the dressing-table. It broke to fragments.

My mind was racing. We intended to discard a lot of furniture when we moved into a smaller house and I was working out which pieces could be smashed without regret.

He turned to me again.

'It was my pound, you know,' I said.

'No, it wasn't. I spent all the money you gave me.'

'If you make a list of what you've spent it on, I'll give you back the pound,' I suggested.

'I bloody well won't make a list.'

'All right. No pound.'

He really did not want to smash anything else.

'I spent two pounds, eleven shillings and twopence,' he said.

'Right. You give me the nine shillings and tenpence change, and I'll give you the pound.'

'After you've given me the pound,' he said.

'No, before.'

He turned to attack the large dressing-table mirror. I thought of the little boys in the next room and I knew they must not be upset. Although violent, he had made little noise and I hoped they were still asleep. I decided I would have to give him the money.

'All right,' I said. 'I'll find the pound.' I searched for it among the bedclothes. Just as I gave it to him, a voice called from downstairs.

'Are you there, John?'

I recognised Bill. John opened the door and called back:

'I'll come down.'

I disentangled myself from the bedclothes, straightened out my dress and followed him down. He was in the kitchen, making a show of sorting garden apples on the table, no sign upon his face of the turmoil he had just left.

'Bill,' I said. 'Will you come up to my bedroom?'

Bill laughed at my request but came upstairs. He looked at the chaotic room without comment, slightly embarrassed. John followed us up.

'Do you think you could help me to get the bed up again?' I asked.

'Of course,' said Bill.

And we laughed. John and Bill righted the bed between them.

'Thank you very much,' said John. 'Does your woman behave like this?' The caveman expression followed aptly upon the caveman behaviour.

I asked Bill to help me heave on the double mattress as it was unlikely that John would help me after he had left. They did it between them. I thanked Bill again, and we all laughed this time, and then went to the front door.

'I hope you're satisfied,' said John grimly as he closed the door behind Bill, and went to watch television. The pound was in his pocket.

Michael helped me to make the bed and told me that he and James had been listening outside the door and ran to get Bill when they feared for my safety. They both went back to their homework looking relieved at my lack of dismay, and I went downstairs to make some coffee. John came out of the sitting-room, and tried with diminished effort to rile me.

'I can't even have a bloody good row, now,' he muttered, defeated. 'Come on, Buster, we're going out.'

'I bet you don't dare leave that pound on the table while you're out.'

'I wouldn't trust you with it.'

'I promise I will leave it there.'

'No, I can't trust you.'

'What you really mean is that you need it to buy yourself a drink.'

'I can't trust you,' he reiterated.

'All right. But we both really know why you're going out.'

He went back to watch television. He wasn't going to admit he wanted a drink. He was caught.

Later, while I was cleaning my teeth, he came into the bathroom and said: 'I hope you're pleased with yourself. You've got your evidence now.'

'I suppose I have. But that wasn't why I asked Bill to come up. I knew I couldn't manage the bed on my own.'

He went back to my bedroom and I heard him tipping the bed over again and banging about. I sat down on the bathroom seat and laughed, genuinely. It was pathetic and funny. He came back to me angrily.

'This is all an act,' he said.

'Of course it's an act. Nobody could behave the way I have without it being an act. But it worked, didn't it?'

'You look ridiculous.'

'I'm lucky. I was born happy.'

'You? You were born with nothing.'

'Nonsense.'

'What do you think you have?'

'Optimism, honesty, a love of life.'

His face was suffused by an intensity of frustrated animosity.

'You reduce me,' he cried. 'How can I gain self-respect if you reduce me?'

'I know. How can you gain any self-respect while I am here to remind you of the past simply by my presence? Why don't you go away for a while and build yourself up where nobody knows you?'

'I've thought about it,' he said. 'I must have a strong masochistic streak which makes me stay.'

'No. You just haven't got the guts to go.'

'You're the one who should go.'

'No. The boys wouldn't want to be left with you.'

And then, for the first time, he agreed with me. And went to bed. I went to my bedroom and found the bed undisturbed. He had simply lifted it and banged it down again; the spirit had gone out of him.

I slumped. I felt as though I had been exorcising the devil. As I had stood and faced him I had repeated over and over to myself the Twenty-third Psalm, the bits I could remember, like an incantation. I could have avoided the confrontation but I had caused it to happen; I could have hidden it from Bill but I had purposely allowed him to witness the results of John's intemperance, and I believed that I had done this with an instinct which knew that, as long as he believed he remained credible as a normal, rational man to outsiders, he would cling to the remnants of self-respect which such illusion of credibility gave him. In order to destroy his fantasy of self-delusion, I had to reveal the Jekyll/Hyde personality clearly to an outsider so that he himself could no longer pretend that it did not exist. For it is the reflection of ourselves we see in another's eyes which persuades us of what we are. We can delude ourselves only so long as we can delude others. Never before had John been exposed to himself with such unarguable clarity. I had not planned the incident but I was glad that it had happened. Surely, now, he could not much longer withstand the pressures that must be forcing themselves on him against his will to seek treatment of his insanity.

As the days grew shorter, John began to talk about our move in the New Year in a way that implied that he did not expect to be with us in the new house. One day, on his bedside table, I found a book of poems open and picked it up to see what he had been reading.

Remember me when I am gone away,
Gone far away into the silent land;
When you can no more hold me by the hand,
Nor I half turn to go yet turning stay.
Remember me when no more day by day
You tell me of our future that you plann'd;
Only remember me; you understand
It will be late to counsel then or pray.
Yet if you should forget me for a while
And afterwards remember, do not grieve;
For if the darkness and corruption leave
A vestige of the thoughts that once I had,
Better by far you should forget and smile
*Than that you should remember and be sad.**

I felt my mouth tremble and the easy tears spring to my eyes. I wondered whether he had left the book open purposely in the hope that I might read it, whether this was the only way that he had of telling me that he knew the distress he caused and understood. I wept then for him and his inability to share his secret, inmost anguish with us. I could not, though, allow the further thought that came to me to develop.

John no longer attempted to hurt me and became yet more withdrawn, living in an isolated, agonised world of his own. When his eyes were not marbled over by cold hate for me and my refusal to be a scapegoat for his wretchedness, the bleakness of his loneliness crept into them and he looked whipped; I longed to take him in my arms and comfort him like a child. But I knew that I could not help him, that I had to show him that we could lead full lives of our own independent of him. If his spirit broke, there was a chance that he would find release from the few remaining shreds of arrogance which prevented him from accepting defeat and that he would admit to himself that his only chance of survival was in the willingness to submit himself to the ignominy of further professional treatment. Guy had told us of an unusually successful alcoholic unit in a hospital which, although not within our area, would probably accept him as a patient, if he would only express his willingness to go. The only barrier to his entry was his own pride. I hoped that some tiny core of under-

* Christina Rossetti, *Remember*.

standing within him realised that we still hoped for him, that he had not driven us from him for ever, and that this might sustain him, but I had no confirmation of this; he saw only our detachment. Perhaps he could not believe in us when so clearly we did not appear to believe in him. His mind was too confused and clouded to be able to separate from our actions that core of faith in his own underlying worth which sustained me, and through me the boys, in our emotional separation from him. James talked little to him because he feared his hurtful remarks, and withdrew into a study of metaphysics, mixing little with the family. Michael, percipient and capable of controlled behaviour, had gained a maturity of understanding but lost his natural exuberance in his determination to maintain a semblance of normality in our household but, at thirteen, such forbearance put great strain upon him. David felt John's pain, and my pain, and longed for everybody to be kind. Each day, as I left for work, he said, 'Don't die, Mummy,' and I knew how deep was his sense of insecurity. Andrew contained his fear within himself, and grew paler and paler. I knew that the time was approaching when I must take some action, for the sake of the children.

One Friday in November, John went up to London. I learnt later that he cashed a dud cheque at our local chemist. All week he had been drinking again and when he came home that day, he was heavy with alcohol. He told me he had been to see his mother. I subsequently telephoned her and she told me that she had given him twenty pounds because he said he had no money. I knew that, with such a large amount of cash in his pocket, the week-end would be disastrous, so I telephoned one of my sisters and asked her to have David and Andrew for the week-end, and asked Pamela Wilson to take James. They both agreed without hesitation. Michael was going out on Saturday with his school cadets and elected to come home afterwards. With the boys away, I could not face a day alone with John and I invited myself to lunch with Diana and Bill. I decided that if, when I got home, John was still drinking, I must start making plans for at least a temporary separation. He came in at eight o'clock that evening, reekingly unsteady. I knew that I would have to stay at home on Monday, not only for the boys but also to give myself time to make urgent arrangements for our future. On Monday morning, I telephoned my office and told my assistant that I should not be coming in. I explained a little of the situation to her and asked her to tell my principal that I would come and see him the next afternoon. I spoke to a London solicitor to whom I had been recommended and made an appointment with him, too. Then I went to see Sylvia. I told her that I suspected that John might be pushed over the brink of his indecision into agreeing to go to hospital and that I felt it was time that Alcoholics Anonymous took over. With his world disintegrating around him the moment may have come for him to acknowledge defeat. She came to see him in the early evening, accompanied by her small boy. John had gone to bed at two o'clock and remained there since. Sylvia went upstairs to his room and I heard him telling her that he was very worried because he did not think that I was capable of looking after the boys, so he could not consider leaving them with me. She came down after a little while and told me she could not get through to him.

Then John came down, dressed to go out.

'So you're running away again,' said Sylvia. 'Where are you going, The Green Man?'

'No,' I said. 'He can't drink at the local pubs because all his friends know about him, so he's joined a working men's club. I expect he's going there.'

John made several moves towards the front door but each time hesitated, as though a part of him wanted to stay and be persuaded. I realised that I must leave him again with Sylvia, who understood so much better than I his state of mind. Had she not suffered those same feelings herself?

I took David and Andrew, with Sylvia's child, into the sitting-room and pulled *Winnie-the-Pooh* out of the bookcase. As I sat on the settee, the children gathered about me, reading what Piglet said to Pooh and how cross Eeyore was when he realised Rabbit could read better than he, I tried not to strain to hear the conversation from the kitchen. Then, after a chapter and a half, the boys gleefully listening to the familiar story unaware of the climactic situation developing which was to affect the lives of us all, Sylvia called me. John was standing subdued.

'John says he would like an appointment with Dr. Townsend,' said Sylvia. Dr. Townsend ran the alcoholic unit which Guy had recommended. Sylvia left, telling me that she would get into touch with other members of AA; John went back to bed, I bathed David and Andrew, and Michael and I had some supper. James was still away.

That night I could not sleep. I feared that John would change his mind overnight. Worried that if I lay in bed allowing indecision to creep in, I should lose the intense clarity with which I suddenly saw what I must do, I got up and went downstairs. I had had some material for some while but never found the time to make it up. At two in the morning, I began laying the pattern for a trouser suit across the cloth, and cut it out before I returned to bed, my tense nerves calmed by irrelevant concentration. I was convinced now that I must keep up the pressure and not allow John to feel any relaxation in my determination. I would not alter my plans because he appeared to have succumbed to the concerted influence of my actions and Sylvia's words; he could so easily relapse into an euphoric sense that his lost security could be retrieved. When I told him the next day that I was going to London, he asked why.

'I'm going to see my solicitor,' I said.

'I see,' was his only reply, but he looked desolate.

I learned from the solicitor that I should be able to get a legal separation within four days, if I could produce evidence. I told him that I could.

'Don't you want to divorce your husband?' he asked.

'No,' I said. 'I don't want anything as final as that. I believe he is going to recover.'

'You have great optimism,' he said.

I smiled. 'I know my husband. I love him.'

He told me that I would be able to get legal aid if I sought further help from him but that he would waive the costs for that interview. He did not believe me when I said that I doubted that I should need to see him again; I had just wanted confirmation of my legal position.

Then I went to my office and spoke to my principal. He was aghast when I told him my story, but helpful and understanding. I told him that I should probably be at work the next day.

I had arranged in the morning for David and Andrew to go to Sylvia after school and stay the night there; Michael was going to my mother for a few days, and James was invited to stay on the rest of the week at the Wilsons. John had clung to the little boys and it was a shock for him when I told him that I was sending them away again. He called on Sylvia while I was in London and insisted that they should come home but she, adept at coping with an alcoholic, prevented his going in to them and upsetting them. When I reached home, he was writing an unhinged letter to her, accusing her of kidnapping them. He came to me and said that she was not capable of looking after her own children, certainly not of caring for his, and I must go round and fetch them home.

'She is perfectly capable and they are happy there,' I said. 'If you feel so strongly about it, why don't you telephone the police?'

He went back to his room, and later came down to say that he had decided not to send the letter. Then he changed his tactics. He informed me that he was going to cook us a wonderful dinner. He peeled sufficient potatoes for six and then went out. When he came back he was carrying a record—one of my favourite Haydn pieces—and said he planned a cosy evening for us. A huge fire was blazing in the sitting-room, only the side lamps were lit. I knew then that I, too, had to get away, for he was trying to soften me.

'I'm not planning to have dinner,' I said, but he continued his preparations. I went upstairs and packed my nightdress and toilet articles into a small bag. The record was playing at full volume. Under cover of the noise, I crept downstairs and let myself quietly out of the front door. Once again, I trespassed upon the hospitality of Diana and Bill. They received me without question. Anxious for John, I stood at their window and wondered what he was doing, and was relieved when I saw a car draw up outside our house and a man get out. I recognised him as an AA member. I telephoned Pamela to tell her where I was and later learnt that Kenneth, too, came to our house that night. Afraid that John might take his own life, he stayed with him until two-thirty in the morning until it was clear that he would probably only sleep.

John arrived on the doorstep while I was dressing the next morning to ask whether I would go back before I went to work so that we could arrange a few matters; Diana told me he had telephoned the night before, after I was asleep, to ask if I was with them. I told him that I was coming in a few minutes to pack some clothes for David and Andrew who were returning to my sister for the rest of the week; I had already telephoned their headmaster the day before to tell him that they would be absent from school. I felt it was essential to keep all the boys away until John had gone and avoid any chance of emotional scenes. I had also spoken to another friend of mine and asked her if I could stay with her. While I was talking to John, telling him of my arrangements, the AA member of the night before turned up and asked me to telephone our doctor so that John's entry into hospital went through correctly. Caught in the intricacies of bureaucratic administration, trying to locate the right person at the hospital, I sat at the desk, telephone in hand, and smoked my way through a whole packet of cigarettes; John became anxious. Now that he had finally surrendered, he seemed to wish for a quick execution of his decision, impatient of the inevitable delay. It was soon too late for me to go to work and John, to my relief, went out; I found it difficult to remain calm in his fretful presence. I guessed that he had gone for a drink but it no longer seemed to matter very much.

I started packing my bag, realising that there was a possibility that John would not be accepted immediately and knowing that I might have to stay away for some time. When he came home after half an hour, I found it difficult to remember what I was doing, for he followed me from room to room. I was sure I was sane, yet, as he talked, I felt my own mind become unhinged. So often he had persuaded me that falsehood was truth, and truth relative anyway, because, in my need for him, I desperately wanted to believe him.

'Are you sure you know what you are doing?' he said.

'Yes.'

'Our life hasn't been all bad, has it?'

'No.'

'Things have got out of proportion lately. But it's not as bad as you make out.'

'It is.'

'Come, darling. You know that it's not all my fault. You are a bit neurotic,' he smiled gently, indulgently.

A buzz started in my head. I felt again the longing to succumb, to say that I was sorry that I was so intolerant, that we would start afresh.

'Why don't you go out for a little while,' I said. 'Buster needs a walk.'

He agreed. He needed another drink.

I threw my remaining clothes into the suitcase and left the house before he came back. I did not dare stay for I might become sorry for him.

My friend, Elizabeth, was still at work when I reached her

house, but she had left the front door key under the mat for me. I let myself in and was moved by gratitude for the thought which had prompted her to leave me a welcoming tray of food before she left that morning. She had forgotten nothing. There was a bottle of sherry, soup, cold sausages, cheese, bread, butter, fruit, coffee, and even a packet of cigarettes with matches beside them. I made myself some coffee and went to the telephone. I had, once again, to inform everybody where I was so that they could contact me—my sister, Pamela Wilson, my mother, Sylvia, my office. And I had to speak to John's mother, to try to convey to her my certainty that the climax had been reached, that now we had all to act with a single-mindedness of purpose so that nobody should convey to John the slightest readiness to provide sanctuary for him. I think she was numbed by shock that her son could have become as he was; she did not understand but she did not interfere.

Over the years of our marriage, we had not drawn closer to John's parents. John rarely contacted them and I, from a sense of duty, was the one who invited them for the rare visit, uncomfortable times which strained us all. His father had died a few years earlier and John gave no indication of grief; I do not know whether he felt any sense of loss. I had avoided telling his mother of the unhappiness in our marriage but I knew that she was conscious of the tension between us when she came to us for the occasional week-end. It had been a relief to tell her of John's alcoholism two years before, when he acknowledged it himself, but since his period in hospital she had not been aware that he had relapsed. I rationalised that I did not wish to worry her with our problems, but I think I was really protecting myself against a sense of responsibility towards her. I did not want to have to bear her distress. She came for a week-end and, unhappy though she was at John's protracted unemployment, neither of us allowed her to learn that he was drinking again. For that week-end, he remained sober. I made light of our reversal of roles, declaring that it was a situation which was becoming more generally acceptable, that people had begun to realise that the conventional attitude that the man should be the breadwinner had no basis in logic. When, a few months later, she was due to come again, at a time when our relationship was perpetually tense and we were utterly estranged, I told John that I could no longer keep from her the knowledge that he was still drinking. I heard him telephone her and tell her that we would have to put off the week-end as I had a heavy cold. I felt only relief. It was with the shock of unpreparedness that she learnt from me, during this last week-end, the true tale of John's deterioration and of his imminent entry once more into hospital. I was fortunate that she did not seek to interfere. Aware of my laxity in the past, I bought a book on alcoholism and sent it to her hoping that she would understand it as a sickness. When she sought my advice on whether she should communicate with John, I could only tell her that I did not know, that I could not be an intermediary between them, that I had no conception of my own husband's feelings towards her; I suggested that she find an Al-Anon group where advice would be disinterested and unemotional. Throughout the next few months, I had no communication with her. She knew where John was; she must make her own decisions. I had my own emotional distress to bear and I had to carry the children through the uncertainties which beset us; I could not carry anyone else. John's brother telephoned me and asked me whether I would meet him, but I refused. I could not talk about our situation; I felt capable only of dealing with practicalities. I knew that if I were obliged to relive the past in an attempt to convey the essence of our unhappy marriage, I would risk my own perilously balanced emotional stability. I could not talk to anybody of John for a while. I could not even think of him to myself.

Sylvia telephoned me that Wednesday evening that I spent in the quiet, uncharged atmosphere of Elizabeth's home, and told me that John had been accepted as a patient by Dr. Townsend and would be leaving the next morning. I sighed a prayer of thankfulness and went to bed, warmed by Elizabeth's undemanding companionship, in the grateful knowledge that AA had taken over and that I could rely on them. The next morning before I went to work, I called in quickly to take the dog for a walk and make sure the house was locked. Two AA members were already there, waiting to drive John to the hospital. He was upstairs, packing his bag.

'I haven't come to interfere,' I said quickly. John came down and looked at me almost without recognition. I did not kiss him.

'Goodbye,' I said, as the three men went out. 'Good luck.'

Chapter Eight

THE BOYS and I stayed away in our separate refuges until the end of the week. We all needed a rest from each other's presence. I called into the house morning and evening, taking the dog back to Elizabeth's house when I returned from work and leaving him at home in the day-time.

I moved back at the week-end before the children came home, to do the shopping for the following week, and began to make arrangements for the boys. I was concerned for Andrew, worried that he and David would get home from school three hours before I arrived home from work. My parents agreed to come and stay with us for a few days while I sought some solution to the problem. I knew that they would give Andrew the love and security that he so desperately needed in his inarticulate unhappiness. His father had given to him the affection that he withheld from the rest of us, for Andrew alone had not been constrained by the need to control the spontaneity of his own love, had not understood the inevitable effect that the reassurance of unjustified trust had on John. He had supported John in his childish inability to comprehend him, but he too had been fearful of his anger. He was a subdued little boy and he sought to reduce his own feeling of fear by befriending, at school, the timorous and afraid. He missed his father and his loss was not alleviated by gladness, as was ours, that we were free of his alternately sullen or turgid presence. We found respite in our necessity to adapt our actions to John's moods and release to be ourselves; Andrew had never ceased to be himself and to give that part of himself which John demanded and, though his burden had been heavy, he missed it and the sadness showed in his pale looks and shadowed eyes. We were all gentle with him.

My parents returned to their own home after two days, when my mother slipped down the stairs and hurt her back. She realised that their presence was more a liability than an asset, for stretched as we all were to the limits of our capacity to relate naturally to each other after the months of unnatural forbearance, we found the presence, even of such anxious, loving people, more than we could endure. Their very anxiety to help became a responsibility on us to respond and my mother, wise woman, quickly realised this. Her accident made their withdrawal simple and saved the need for discussion of its wisdom. By the end of the week we had evolved a way of living which we felt we could all manage. On Saturday, at lunch-time, little Andrew lay his head upon the table and said: 'I'm sad.' Suddenly I realised that we were all trying to be too gentle with each other.

'This is ridiculous,' I said. 'We all go around like ghosts because Daddy has gone away. We shouldn't be sad. We should be glad. We know he is ill and that we cannot help him, and now he is in hospital and being helped by people who can, so we should all be happy.'

Michael quickly caught up my attempt to brace our spirits and rallied to our need to be cheerful. And so we became and learnt to live as a co-operating family. James took responsibility for feeding and exercising the dog and for bringing in the fuel for the stove and the fire. Michael came home from school each day and made the tea and sent the little boys to bath before I came home. Each day I telephoned from the office at tea-time to check that all was well and he always said it was. When I reached home David and Andrew were in their dressing-gowns and I would chat with them and see them into bed before getting supper for the rest of us. I was glad it was winter-time for there was no inducement for them to roam out. I hated having latchkey children but they all demonstrated their own sense of responsibility and gave me no cause for alarm.

We had an elderly aunt living nearby who was concerned for us and anxious to help, but the boys found that she confused them. For a short while we took up her offer to come in to look after them until I came home, but it was not a success. Michael said that she was a muddler and David and Andrew declared that things went much more smoothly when she was not there. We did not wish to hurt her feelings but when, one day, I telephoned home to be told that Michael had not yet arrived, I realised that my aunt was worrying about what might have happened to him and conveying her anxiety to the little boys. I spoke to David and told him that I had remembered that

Michael had shooting practice that evening. David asked me frantically to ask my aunt to let him get the tea himself; she was upsetting him. Over the telephone, I tried to organise them all, and Michael rang me back twenty minutes later to say that he was home. We realised that we must tactfully dispense with my aunt's services.

We had many telephone calls during the early days of John's departure and Michael became the filter through which I received them. I would speak to my practical friends and was grateful to them for their help, but I avoided the sympathetic ones; I had no wish for sympathy and found it demoralising. I had to protect myself from the over-solicitous or the unintelligent, and concentrate on the details of our daily living. I did not want to speak of John to anybody, particularly his old drinking friends. I did not consciously think of John at all. I did not go to see him in hospital because I knew that, perched as I was on the edge of physical endurance, my feelings lashed down tightly in some inner secret hold which I could not yet explore, I risked tumultuous, annihilating ruin to the steadiness of my mind in dealing with the day-to-day effort of existence with the boys if I allowed the slightest unleashing of my emotions. I was determined to survive and I knew the terms of my survival: they rejected any exposure to normal, human feelings. One evening, after I had been conscious of an unformulated ache which I could not allow myself to recognise as a longing for his arms, his humour, his need of me, I imagined, as I stood at the kitchen sink peeling potatoes for the following day, that I heard his footsteps coming up the path. My stomach clenched with fear of his return and the lies and the plausibility and the necessity to brace myself against him. I was not yet ready to have him close to me, and I knew that he could not be ready, that he could not yet have learnt to know himself and give without demand, without using my compliance and my need for him to assert himself. It was not him and I was relieved, and knew that I was right in my decision not to visit him. We both needed time to regain ourselves.

During the first month of his absence, I felt a clarity of purpose which buoyed me up and carried me through the excessive physical effort needed to maintain our home with some semblance of decency so that we did not become squalid, to share with the boys their enthusiasms and their childish upsets so that they should not feel neglected, and to remain alert and effective in my job so that my employers did not observe any deterioration in my work. I found that the intensity of my will to ignore the deep insecurity I felt in my relationship with John, the uncertainty I had of how he felt towards me, created a strangely elevated certainty of my ability to abstract from life only the important issues of living each day. This sharpness of my recognition of the priorities created a veneer of undefeatedness and the unspoken admiration of my close friends at my refusal to acknowledge possible failure and gave me back an image of myself which I found pleasing and which augmented my own belief. I did not know what the future held but I found a sharpness and sweetness in the present, unmuddied by John's indecision and power to project on to me his own uncertainties. I developed what I liked to think was a panache which protected me against doubt and fear and the misunderstanding of well-meaning people who did not know the depth of my inner caring for John. When one acquaintance, who knew something of alcoholism, said to me: 'Do you think you'll ever see John again?' she could not know the agonising exposure she caused to the closely covered wound in the depths of my being; she saw only the shield of defiance I help up to the world against intrusion of feeling. My refusal to speak of him meant that I did not care.

I turned to books for my comfort when I felt despair creep in and I found a passage in Benjamin Disraeli which supported me.

> There are tumults of the mind, when, like the great convulsions of nature, all seems anarchy and returning chaos, yet often, in those moments of vast disturbance, as in the material strife itself, some new principle of order, or some new impulse of conduct, develops itself, and controls, and regulates, and brings to an harmonious consequence, passions and elements which seemed only to threaten despair and subversion.*

I liked to think that some new principle of order, some new impulse of conduct was emerging for John, but it was not until January that I felt able to impinge myself upon his awareness, to try to convey to him some knowledge of my own conflict.

We had had little contact. We had written businesslike letters to each other on the disposal of the house but they held small element of the personal. He kept me informed of his progress from the main hospital into the alcoholic unit after the initial

* Benjamin Disraeli, *Sybil.*

introductory period of withdrawal. I wrote to him of the boys and reassured him of our well-being though he showed no anxiety, and I realised that he was turned inward upon himself. I learnt that there was great emphasis on group therapy in the unit and that the essential requirement of the course was absolute honesty. After a few weeks he had to write his life history and present it to the group for discussion; he seemed fearful of what he would reveal to himself. With my wish to encourage him with a sense of hope, I copied out another quotation, this time from Thomas Mann, and sent it to him:

> The bright and cheery possibilities of life only reveal themselves after that truly cleansing catastrophe which is correctly called social ruin, and the most hopeful situation in life is when things are going so badly for us that they can't possibly go worse.*

As our exchange of letters grew less stilted and more friendly, feelings emerged again. We had spent Christmas apart. My own instinct was that to visit John while he was undergoing emotional upheaval could only create tension in all of us, that we must leave him alone to cope with what I hoped was his increasing ability to relate to other people in a less sensitised way so that he did not feel a personal affront upon his dignity whenever he felt himself impugned, incapable of distinguishing between the objective and the subjective, like a child unable to separate the personal from the impersonal, his needs from the needs of others. But I did not wish to impose my own inclination upon the children, and deny them their father's company at this conventional time of family gathering if they desired it. To James, and Michael, and David, I put the question:

'Do you want to visit Daddy over Christmas? Don't say what you think you ought to say. Say what you really want.'

'No,' they each replied.

We did not ask Andrew, perhaps knowing he would say yes. There seemed no reason to give him the opportunity and then deny him. I told John of our decision over the telephone, and he accepted it without apparent hurt. He wrote later that he was sure that this was wise, having seen the highly charged atmosphere that resulted when other people's families visited them. 'Dr. Townsend takes the view', he added, 'that this disease is

* Thomas Mann, *Confessions of Felix Krull, Confidence Man.*

very much a family affair, hence the reason we are encouraged to discuss the family aspect of our social relationships at length in our group therapy sessions.'

I had my first contact with the hospital in early January, when the psychiatric social worker invited me to meet her. For the first time I had to uncover the feelings which I had allowed to lie dormant for so long and give some indication of my attitude towards John. After two hours with her, recounting my own version of the story of the years of our married life with all its distresses and deceits and the awful lack of genuine communication, I was drained, incapable any longer of maintaining my tight control of emotion. The next morning, I could not cope with my usual equanimity with the small crises which invariably occurred as we all hurried through the small tasks preparatory to our departure for school and work. The boys were subdued in their anxiety not to upset me.

'Don't die, Mummy,' said David, as he kissed me goodbye, and his concern was so evident that I was ashamed of the lack of control which had led me to scream at Michael when he dropped a packet of porridge oats.

All the way to my office, as I hurried down the street to the station, as I sat on my commuter train, as I stood unseeingly on the escalator down to the Tube, I was obsessed by the need to write to John and tell him what I felt for him, to convey to him my own insecurity in my ignorance of him, to make him aware of me as a living, suffering human being held hanging in an abyss of uncertainty upon his inchoate love for me. I reached my office and flung off my coat, relieved to find nobody there. I sat down at my typewriter and rolled a piece of paper into the machine.

Dear John,

Now that you are half-way through your course, obviously we have got to start thinking about the future. I don't know what plans you have, or whether you have any. I don't know whether or not you want to come back to us or whether you prefer to strike out on your own or with somebody else. I know nothing about your feelings. I do know that I can never go back to the life we have lived. I cannot ever again live with lies, whether they be trivial (like pretending something you've cooked is homemade and then finding the container you bought it in in the wastepaper), to not admitting you've had a drink, to spending other people's money, to not admitting anything. Over the past months while you've been at home, every time I have tried to make you talk you've clammed up. And this is what marriage to you has been like. Never knowing whether you are telling the truth, never being able to talk frankly about our problems, never really knowing you at all.

I would like very much to read your life history, and you know that if you wish me to there is no reason why I shouldn't. Only you can make it as confidential as that. If you choose not to let me, I can only conclude that there is a lot you have not mentioned, because you must know that I accept the past, know more or less all the terrible things that have happened, so it can't be to protect me that you wouldn't want me to read it but to protect yourself from my knowledge that you are not coming clean about it. I have accepted that there has been constant deceit from the first year of our marriage, possible adultery, and this does not frighten me. The only thing that frightens me is the fact that you may still be deluding yourself and if you are doing that, I don't see how you can possibly begin to live life truthfully and fully and happily and how you will manage without the illusory comfort of alcohol. And if you need that, we cannot have you back.

I have spoken to James and Michael. James, who is so very insecure, finds it harder to accept you than Michael, who is less self-centred and has a warmth in him that somehow James so far cannot release in himself. The little ones, obviously, I do not talk to so much because they are too young. They love you and that's it. They understand that you are sick, and if I tell them that you are never going to recover from this sickness then you will gradually fade from their memory. James says he is so used to being without a proper father (because he's never had one) that he doesn't care very much, but the boy is terribly hurt inside I think.

As for me, I still love you and I can scarcely bear it. I think we must meet fairly soon to discuss the future—if there is to be a future. I would like to meet you for a day away from the children and any interruption to really hard talking. Perhaps next week. By that time, you will have presented your life history. I hope you decide to let me see it too, perhaps before we meet, so that I can get some idea of what stage of acceptance of yourself as you are you have reached. Also I must discuss finance with you and what is to happen to the spare cash that will be released by the sale of the house.

Maybe all this is irrelevant because you don't want us any longer. How can I know if you never say anything?

Please write soon.

Love

Mary.

He wrote back immediately.

Dear Mary,

Yes, of course I want you all and I want you to know this right away—I also want you to know that I still love you too.

I am due to read my life story next week and to be cross-examined by the group and the staff for the whole of that week, so I am in too much of a turmoil to take in and reply fully to all the points you raised in your very candid letter.

I shall be much clearer in my mind in ten days' time and I am sure, and indeed have been advised by the group with whom I have discussed your letter, that I should wait until then to give you my thoughts on it.

All my love.

John.

I was comforted by his urgent response to my need for recognition, I appreciated the obvious sense of his discussing my letter with the people who were trying to help him in their professional understanding or in their identification with him as another alcoholic, but I felt a stir of anguish at the thought of my most intimate communication with him being subjected to discussion and analysis, held to the light of cold, dispassionate consideration of its true meaning. I felt shut out, but knew that I had myself chosen to be shut out. Of my own decision I had refused to be involved in John's inquisition, to expose myself to criticism as he was exposing himself in his search for his own identity. I was alone and in my loneliness I turned to Pamela Wilson. I had kept a copy of my letter—I kept copies of everything, a habit born out of distrust. John had denied so much that I felt my need to hold on to reality must be fed by written confirmation of the truth as it appeared to me, that no distortion of my perception must be allowed to creep in through the passing of time and accurate memory. I had a passion for writing things down and in the writing purged from my soul the bitterness which I knew must gain no hold on me if I were to retain a clear vision of the ultimate supremacy of good. Truth was my talisman and in my refusal to accept anything but truth perhaps I lost all compassion and flogged John with the same whip that I used on myself. I refused to blur the edges of my own interpretation of truth.

I went to Pamela one evening after the boys were fed and settled and took my letter with me for her to read, as well as the other letters which John and I had written to each other, so that she should know the state of our relationship. I wanted her to tell me what to do, to make my decisions for me. For the first time since John's entry into hospital I wept my desolation to somebody else, and poured into her ears the truth of my loneliness. She gripped my hand as I shuddered out the resentment that burned in me against John's laying bare to others my inmost self, the self that he alone saw, with distorted vision, and I admitted my need too to expose him. I also required the emotional support which he was finding, and to be told of my own fallibility.

'John is going to be different when he comes out of hospital, and you'll have to change too,' she said.

She did not treat me with the ruthless refusal to allow any of my self-delusions to go unremarked with which I had treated John, but she saw the weakness in me of pride and arrogance in my own righteousness and she was wise in her discernment. She left me to discover for myself the meaning of her comment.

I returned home feeling a little less constricted by the tension of holding myself taut against compassion. Her concern for me warmed me and her willingness to be involved in my troubles without morbid curiosity, only desiring to find a way to convey to me, without hurt, my own need for self-awareness and tolerance gave me a sense of the worth of her friendship. I began to realise that perhaps I deceived myself more than others by the mask of capability and self-sufficiency that I wore. I recognised the insight of George Eliot when she wrote:

> Examine your words well, and you will find that even when you have no motive to be false, it is a very hard thing to say the exact truth, even about your own immediate feelings—much harder than to say something fine about them which is *not* the exact truth.*

* George Eliot, *Adam Bede*.

How often had I pretended to an acceptance of our condition which bore no resentment, yet did I not nurse a secret belief that it was only because of John and his behaviour that I was unable to develop a genuine love of others, a quality which I saw and envied in some of my friends. I excused myself that my life was too busy and my own problems too manifold for me to pay more than cursory attention and give more than superficial interest to the sorrows and disasters of the world, but was I not innately selfish? I knew that John, in his true self, unhindered by his addiction, was naturally kinder than I.

He telephoned to tell me that he had been told that he might come home at the week-end for a day: would I be prepared to have him? I said yes and mixed with my gladness at the thought of his being with us in the family again was fear. I was frightened to meet this new John, of taking up our relationship again, afraid that I might release in him the old antagonisms or find a stranger, who had grown so apart from me that there was no point of recognition, no mutual common base upon which we could begin to build a new understanding. The night before, I lay in bed seeking some certainty of how I should behave. I had knelt and prayed to the God I now believed in but was unable to define. I prayed often now and sometimes found release in seeking to subjugate my will to an influence which I was sure existed beyond me and outside me if only I could forget my own petty desires and learn to bow to a greater wisdom than any I could hope to find in myself. My prayers that night did nothing to relieve the uncertainty within me, and I got into bed with all the trepidation of my probable inadequacy to meet John with a spontaneity of love which would make no demands upon him. Seeking to divert my mind and forget my anxiety, I turned to the bookcase beside my bed and pulled out a copy of the *New English Bible*. I knew that humility was a virtue which I found constantly evading my best intentions and thought to turn to the Gospels for guidance. The pages opened and my eyes fell upon a verse in James:

> What a huge stack of timber can be set ablaze by the tiniest spark! And the tongue is in effect a fire. It represents among our members the world with all its wickedness; it pollutes our whole being; it keeps the wheel of our existence red-hot, and its flames are fed by hell. Beasts and birds of every kind,

creatures that crawl on the ground or swim in the sea, can be subdued and have been subdued by mankind; but no man can subdue the tongue. It is an intractable evil, charged with deadly venom.*

And I knew then that here was my answer. I had only to guard my tongue and I need not fear. I turned to sleep in the confidence that I should now rest.

I was glad that I had read that passage the following day. When John came to us we saw him again with the eyes of love, and as the day proceeded I was conscious of the change in him, of his determination that the day should be happy. He was less boisterous than of old and there was a new thoughtfulness upon him, as though he were observant of himself, not with the old guarded watchfulness that separated him from us and refused to be drawn in or allow us near but with a willingness to talk in a way that did not seek our approval. He told me of his group and how it sought to unravel the tangled threads of guilt and self-contempt and despair which bedevil the mind of an alcoholic, how it uncovered by identification one with another the qualities to be nurtured and allowed them to grow by weeding out the self-delusions. The going was tough and many did not stay the course, unable to face the relentless battering against the defences they had built up within themselves and against others to a recognition and acknowledgement of their own weakness. In the group, they began to learn to know their own reactions to different situations and where they were destructive to question the cause of their need to create tension which could only be relieved by alcohol. John said that he had learnt that he was emotionally immature. Such candour was a new phenomenon.

'Dr. Townsend says that alcoholism is a disease which affects the whole family,' he stated, as though for him this was an amazing revelation.

I bit off my impulse to say: 'Have you only just realised that?' in amazement at his incredible obtuseness. Instead, I simply agreed with him, glad that he at last understood, and grateful that I had not given way to my base desire to prove to him that I, at least, had been starkly aware of the destructive force of his behaviour for years.

He held me in his arms before he went, and the tenderness in

* James 3: 6–8.

him and the gentleness in his eyes for me unloosed the hard knot of detachment within me which had constricted me for so long. After he left, there was a lightness upon all of us which made us gay, and we looked forward with unbounded joy to his next visit. But later, as I sat alone, I felt again a longing for him and hated Dr. Townsend that he had not allowed him home for the whole week-end that we might find again fulfilment in each other through our bodies. There was a homesick emptiness between my thighs that would not be denied; my breasts nagged with desire for his touch; my throat was dry with craving for him. I lay awake that night unable to quieten the intensity of my need for him.

The following week-end he stayed for the night. Again we had a happy day, marred only by small frictions which we both saw the need to back away from before the searing heat of self-assertion turned them into solid walls of flame which would once again alienate us, leaving only the ashen waste of failure between us. Again, he spoke much of his group and of Dr. Townsend.

'We must not apportion blame,' John quoted, and I felt anger rise in me. Did he think I might start accusing him after all these months of rigid self-control? I clamped my teeth against my tongue and remained silent.

Speaking of what we had lost, he said blithely:

'But it's not so bad, is it? After all, you're doing what you really want to do and have a job. You always said you hated being a housewife.'

'You may be right,' I replied. 'But it's hardly for you to say, is it?' I could not resist replying.

For a moment, his eyes became opaque, but he said no more and went to sweep the garden path. When he came in for tea, the ugly moment of potential acrimony had passed.

When we went to bed, together for the first time after months of separation, I knew that I must not expect him to make love to me. He needed time. But as we lay together he began to stroke me and I felt the tightness in my throat of rising sexual desire.

'I'm tired,' he said, and settled himself for sleep. 'I'm sorry. I can't make love to you tonight.'

'It doesn't matter,' I said, swallowing my disappointment.

But I woke up later out of a dream, crying aloud because in it John had flaunted before me a woman he said was his mistress.

He woke to my shouts of 'No, no!' and took me in his arms to quieten me.

'Have you made love to other women?' I asked, unable to deny the imperative insistence with which this question rose up against my conscious will when I slept.

He was drowsy and his mind, befogged by sleep, was unable to summon the clarity of thought which would, perhaps, have prevented him from revealing himself. He was learning the habit of honesty, too, and the necessity of facing the truth with courage. Perhaps, also, he felt the need to assert to me his virility, of which I had so little evidence.

'Yes,' he said. 'Yes, yes, yes.'

I felt as though I had been physically struck: my flesh flinched from this new blow. I had thought I had faced and overcome my fear of his infidelity but now, face to face with his spoken confirmation, I sickened and became weak with the brutality of his honesty. I lay, immobile, absorbing the hurt.

'Do you think you will do it again?' I said.

'I don't know,' he said.

'I don't think I could live with you if you have affairs,' I said.

He held me tight.

'I don't expect I will.'

There seemed to be a cruelty in him that rejected my need for reassurance.

'Why don't you try to talk about it, to let your feelings out?' he said. 'Why don't you ever show anger? Where does your anger go?'

'I have no anger,' I said. 'Only pain. Do you remember when you used to say that we couldn't afford to go out? And all the time you were having other women? Did you give them presents? What were they like?'

'Placid,' he said.

I lay and thought about this.

'Did you tell them about me?'

'No.'

'Did you laugh that great laugh you used to give when we had both enjoyed it?'

I buried my face in the pillow, trying to stifle the jealousy which flooded through me as I realised that I had had nothing, nothing. 'I thought that that alone was mine. I thought that that was something we had shared and clung to the memory that no-one else had ever shared it with you—not since our marriage. That was really mine.'

He was powerless against my weeping, and he became silent.

'You are too idealistic,' he said, after a while. 'You cannot permit human weakness. Those affairs were nothing to me, nothing. Don't you understand that?'

'Didn't you know you were hurting me?'

'Not if you didn't know.'

'But I could never have an affair with another man. While you have been in hospital, I was asked to meet a man who said he would like to talk to me because his wife was an alcoholic, too, and he was alone. I refused. I did not dare because I knew that, in my loneliness, I might be tempted to seek his love. I knew he was attractive. But I didn't want to hurt you.'

'Oh, Mary,' he cried. 'Stop torturing yourself. It's over, it's past, and will probably never happen again. I wish I hadn't told you. I was a fool to have told you. Now go to sleep and we'll talk about it in the morning.'

'I cannot sleep,' I cried. 'How can I sleep?'

'Well, I can, and I'm going to.'

I lay and stared into the dark.

I woke, surprised that I had slept at all, before six o'clock and went downstairs. I made a cup of coffee and lit a cigarette and tried to tussle with my new pain. I prayed for acceptance of this further revelation of John's betrayal of everything I had believed in. I longed for alleviation of the intensity of my distress, to kill it with drugs, with drink, with loss of consciousness. I took the washing from the laundry basket and wrung out the socks and jerseys, seeking relief in physical activity. I made some tea and took it upstairs, and crawled back into bed. He held me again, and we talked fruitlessly, John trying to explain to me my own feelings and each of his attempts to analyse me twisted the screw of my anguish tighter. He seemed immune from my suffering, separate in his determination not to allow himself to feel with me. And yet I knew that he, who had caused me to suffer, must hold himself aloof lest I pull him into the turbulence of my emotion and evoke the guilt which he had to reject in order to maintain his own stability, that it should not again submerge him.

The day was dreary. John told the boys that I had had a big

shock about something in the past and they must not worry me. I cooked a poor lunch and wasted the day, nursing my pain. I was glad when he went away to catch his bus back to the hospital in the afternoon. I could not bear him near me. I knew that the only way he could comfort me was to make love to me, to allow me to regain him for himself, and this he could not do. He too suffered, aware of my physical need for him and incapable of gratifying it. And yet, when he went, I was desolate.

The next morning, I awoke feeling sick. Several people in my department had gastric influenza and I feared that I had caught it too. I told myself that I had not time to be ill and while I concentrated on my work I was able to ignore the discomfort in my stomach. But the pain came back when I stopped work and was still with me the next day. I could not eat at all. I had another appointment with the psychiatric social worker that afternoon, and when I saw her I told her that I thought I might have something catching, to keep her distance from me. I told her about John's admission of adultery and how I needed to get it in perspective. She informed me that a group of relatives to the patients in the hospital met once a week and suggested that I might like to talk about my feelings there, to learn to understand them and know whether I could accept my new knowledge. John was due to be discharged in two weeks, and we were to move house a week before he came out of hospital. He was to come home the following week-end again and would help me lift the carpets and pack the household goods. I needed his assistance, I could not manage alone, and yet I dreaded his presence. I believed we had the chance of a life unfettered by our memory of the past, because we had both learnt that to hold the resentment and guilt born of past actions pendent over the present mangled the here and now of to-day, but I feared my ability to live by this new precept, that now, with my long-sought goal so near, it was I who might stumble and fall through the unwillingness and incapacity to forgive. I needed time. I knew that, with time, the pain would fade and, like all the other pains, be forgotten, but I was not to be given the time. The sickness within me mounted. I could not forget the joy I had felt in our consummation so long ago, nor hide from the vividness of the picture I bore in my mind of his body locked with some other woman; had she stroked his hair and held his head against her breasts, had he murmured those words of endearment as his hands searched out her soft, yielding flesh. Yes, shrieked the answer in my head, yes, yes, yes. Would he ever want me again? He was lean now, and beautiful, and I was so wan, and thin, and ugly.

I called on Pamela Wilson on my way home, but I did not tell her of John. She said that I looked ill, and I told her that I could not eat, that I was sick but it would pass.

I knew, when I got home, that I must talk to somebody. I thought of Sylvia, who lived nearby: she was an alcoholic too and would understand that I was not betraying John by speaking of his infidelity. She had heard many alcoholics speak of their moral lapses. I waited until the boys were in bed and then went to her. She knew immediately that it was sex that was upsetting me. She said that it was obvious that John liked women. I was amazed; I had never seen other woman's attractiveness to him. He never flirted in my presence and showed no interest in their femininity. She told me that John had tried to make a pass at her when she drove him to a meeting but that she had said that this was not why she took him in her car. She thought that it was a pity that I had never had an affair, that it might have done me good. I explained that I could not, that I believed that it would be hurtful, that I was too intense to dally lightly.

'Do you think you don't attract men?'

'No,' I said. 'I know I do. But if I broke faith with my own integrity, I could not live with myself.'

'That night I came to your house,' she said, 'John told me that he could never make love to you except as a tart. I told him to do just that. It might help.'

I recoiled from her lack of finesse, but I blundered on in my search for perspective. I realised that he had been drunk that night, that he didn't know what he was saying, but I also remembered the old saying: *In vino veritas.* I tried to hide my recoil from the bluntness of her speech.

'I'm frightened of myself when he comes home. I'm randy with sex. The more he knows how much I want him, the less he will be able to pretend he wants me. I can't bear the thought of sleeping with him, but if we sleep separately the boys will feel something is wrong.'

'It's a common problem with alcoholics, you know. But it's harder for a man than a woman; a woman can pretend. You shouldn't worry about John's affairs; they were probably no more to him than going to the lavatory.'

I was unaccustomed to such crude realism and it shocked me. I regretted my impulse to seek Sylvia's help.

Her husband came home and greeted me as he came in.

'You look as though you could do with a drink,' he said, and poured me a large whisky. We talked of other things, and he refilled my glass. When I went home, I was drunk, but the pain was still there. I lit a cigarette and paced round and round the kitchen. It was unbearable. I must telephone John. It was after midnight but I did not care. A woman answered the telephone but expressed no surprise at my demand that she fetch John from his bed. I said into the mouthpiece:

'I'm drunk, and I can't bear it any longer. I can't bear it. I don't know what to do. Nothing is worth anything any more.'

He tried to calm me but I wept and shrieked into the telephone how much I hurt. I told him how he had never given me an engagement ring and then produced a diamond one at Christmas years later when he was drunk and how it meant nothing to me. It was too late. All the time he had been deceiving me and I hated him for it; all the effort and endurance and patience and trying to accept was worth nothing. I had nothing to hold on to any more.

'Stop, stop, Mary,' he cried. 'You are being cruel and wicked.'

'It's not wicked,' I shouted. 'You tell me I should let my anger out and when I do you call me cruel and wicked.'

'Yes, yes,' he placated. 'I'm sorry. But I don't know what to do. What can I do?'

'Nothing,' I said.

'I really do love you.'

'I don't believe you. How can anyone love, and deceive the way you have?'

I forgot all the carefully built reserve I had learnt and my emotion and frustration and bitterness flooded through. I could not put down the telephone, I clung to it as though it were his arm clamped to me, my last defence against disintegration. In the end, he replaced his own receiver and I dragged myself back into the kitchen. I thought that I would faint. Some time later, I stumbled to bed and slept the sleep of exhaustion.

At five-thirty, when I awoke, I was still impaled upon my stricken self, my stomach laden with the spew of undigested grief, mixed as it was with lambent desire. I did not want revenge, only to quicken his lust for me and this I doubted that I could do.

Yet only by fulfilling himself in me could he expunge the past and expiate his crime against my feminine viability. He had to penetrate and stake his claim upon my body before I could feel secure in his love again. I knew his companionship would not be sufficient. I knew I could survive without him, but I was uncertain that I could endure to live with him.

Chapter Nine

WITH THE move to the new house imminent, I had to lay aside my affliction and suppress the knowledge, for the time being, that there was a fresh hazard for me, jealousy. Never before had I known what jealousy really was because I had not consciously felt that I was at risk, so well had John disguised his interest in other women. It made its impact one Saturday afternoon, two days before we moved, when John was at home and we were both too immersed in the active work of packing up the contents of all our rooms to have time to fret about our feelings. I had taken five days' holiday from the office to enable me to finish sorting the detritus of household goods accumulated over the years. I had lived there since I was six years old and though I had imagined that I did not hoard, I was appalled by the amount of useless paraphernalia we had collected. For the past two days I had been making decisions about what to take, what to sell, what to give away, and what to throw out. As we turned out drawers and pulled cupboards away from walls, I could not help noticing how squalid we had become. There had been little time for housework over the past few months and now the neglect showed shamefully. Fortunately it did not matter; nobody else was coming to occupy the house, the whole lot would disappear under the blows of the demolition men. John and I were both dirty, dishevelled and tired when a friend of mine, passing through the district, knocked on the door to inquire how we both were. We sat down and gave her a cup of tea, glad to be able to relax for a short while in the company of an outsider. She was a pretty little thing, intelligent and clever, who yet managed to retain an engaging femininity, her hair long, and fair, and soft, her expression appealing with a wide mouth which curved up at the edges. As we sat and talked, I wondered whether John found her attractive, whether he was comparing my old, worn looks with her young freshness. When she left, she reached up and kissed him goodbye and I was conscious that she felt for him a loving compassion which she had never shown for me. I was angry that he should gain her sympathy and wanted to debase him in her eyes, to tell her about his adultery, to make her feel that, perhaps, I too was deserving of some love and understanding.

John left us to return to the hospital the following day, and on the Monday morning we all awoke early to snatch a quick breakfast before the removal men arrived. One of my sisters came to help and by midday the house was bereft, an empty shell save for the pile of discarded books and broken china and useless implements that we had retained over the years in the vague hope that we should one day get around to repairing them. My sister, whose childhood home it had also been, and I wandered singly around the rooms, extracting the last vestiges of memory before it was all destroyed, but I felt very little then. When we reached the new house, my overwhelming impression was one of confinement. All the furniture seemed too big, we had overestimated its capacity. The removal men dumped the contents of their van and left us, exhausted, scarcely capable of making a cup of tea. James and Michael both had heavy colds and felt wretched, but my other sister had taken David and Andrew to stay with her for a couple of nights to relieve us of having to make all the beds and cope with their inevitable excitement too. I stayed at home the next day and began the task of settling in, but had to return to work the day after. It was my birthday but we all forgot; only later in the morning did I have a contrite telephone call from the boys to wish me many happy returns, and then John telephoned from the hospital to let me know that he, too, had remembered. It seemed unimportant. The evening was gloomy. I reached home to find James and Michael miserable in their confinement, on a cold day, uneasy in an unfamiliar house which had not yet acquired any feeling of home, with the discomfort of thick heads and swollen noses. As we sat eating a hastily prepared supper, James burst out: 'I hate this house.'

In fact, it was not a bad house; it was not even a small house by many standards but the rooms were much smaller than those to which we had been accustomed and we all felt constricted by the low ceilings. I was exhausted by the move after so many weeks of physical strain and psychological tension and I realised that I was near to breakdown. I began to behave in an hysterical manner, and telephoned John at one-thirty that night because I could not sleep. The next morning, he telephoned me and, for the first time, showed anxiety about me. To my relief, he told me that he was definitely being discharged from hospital that weekend and would be with us to help with the laying of carpets and the lugging around of furniture. I no longer cared about his feelings for me for I had convinced myself that he had none, only a sense of duty, but at least this meant that he would take some of the load off me.

I went back to the old house to look for a carpet sweeper and some garden shears which we had left, forgotten, in the cupboard under the stairs but they had gone: the scavengers had already been in. As I got back into my sister's car to drive away, I looked back for the last time. I remembered the day we were married and the walk down the front path, flanked by guests, as we left for our honeymoon, but then I realised it was not the reality I was remembering but the print of one of the wedding photographs. The memories which I really felt emotionally hardly included John: the big bay of the drawing-room window reminded me of our teenage parties and Postman's Knock behind the velvet curtains; the dormer window of my father and mother leaning out to wave goodbye to all of us as we went off on holiday; the bedroom windows of the births of Michael, David and Andrew all born enjoyably at home, and the little dressing-room over the porch, where Michael had slept as a baby, of when I had stood at the window dropping tears upon his face as I held him in my arms to lull him to sleep and waited miserably for John to come home. I did not go back to the house again and it was only several weeks later when John mentioned that he and James had been back to have a look at the demolition that I realised the extent of my attachment to it; I was shocked that they should be so callous. Unable to contain my distress, I went up to our bedroom and lay upon the bed. I felt trapped in this new house, it closed in on me, the bedroom was like a box, and I turned my head to look out of the window to try to achieve a sense of space and saw only the ugly sodium street light outside, higher than the house. Opposite were other houses, all exactly the same with the neat front gardens and tidy, net-curtained windows. I wanted space and light and freedom, not respectable confinement.

John came home at the end of the week of our move and our first night was terrible. He was obviously tired, but he allowed the boys to show him around, to display their new rooms to him and introduce him to discoveries in the garden. He went to bed soon after they did, disappointing me for I had hoped that he would talk once we were alone, but when I followed him up I found him already asleep. I dozed for a while but the Saturday night traffic was disturbing and by two o'clock I could no longer bear to lie wakeful and hear his steady breathing beside me, so I got up and went down to the kitchen and prepared the vegetables for our Sunday lunch and made a cake and did some ironing. At four o'clock I decided to have a bath to see if that would relax me but then John wandered sleepily and grumpily into the bathroom while I was drying myself and asked me what I was doing. I told him I could not sleep so thought to occupy myself usefully. He was annoyed at my desire to talk in the middle of the night and was not at all understanding about my need for reassurance from him, unwilling to accept my statement that he was secure because he knew that I would never let him down and that I loved him whereas I was hopelessly insecure because I had no such certainty. He told me that I was selfish, and I believed he was right; I also believed that he did not like me much.

All through the next day he was hard and looked at me with marbled eyes, giving nothing of himself, and we both concentrated on our own affairs. John planned to spend two weeks cutting and fitting our old carpets into the new house and generally organising some order into its rooms and then turn to the problem of finding a job. I acquiesced and was glad to note a resolve and determination in his manner which had not been apparent when he came out of hospital the previous time. There were many occasions when a solid wall of incomprehension came up between us but we were learning to live together yet apart, each acquiring an ability to cut off from the other rather than let a row develop. Already, the boys at least were responding to the new control in John, becoming less watchful of him as he gained their confidence in him.

He had not shown me his life history, but I knew he had brought the manuscript home from the hospital; I was so uncertain of his feelings towards me that I could not rest until I had read it. I had to know whether he really did hate me, as I suspected, and had simply come back to us for the children's sake before I could decide whether the uncertain, vulnerable life we led was going to prove, in the end, worth the effort. It was clear that he was not going to show it to me voluntarily so I stole it from his pocket one afternoon when he was out and sat in the bedroom reading it. It told me little I did not already know and amazed me more by what was omitted than what was included. His references to me at least were all friendly, and I was relieved. When he came in, not wishing to conceal anything from him, I told him I had read it and he accepted my underhand action without comment.

Because I was so tired, I knew that I had little chance of becoming easy-tempered unless I left them all for a few days, for now that I no longer carried all the responsibility, my body had reacted and all the strength left me. With John's encouragement, I telephoned my old friend Joan and asked her if I could come and stay with her for a week-end and she responded with her usual warm enthusiasm. When I left home the morning of my visit north, John said as I wished him goodbye:

'I expect I shall miss you.'

'I hope so,' I said.

We both wanted to come closer but we did not know how.

My days with Joan were good and rejuvenating and she laughed me into a new attitude towards John. I told her of the shock I had had when I learnt of his infidelity but she treated the matter lightly, refusing to allow me to enjoy my self-indulgent wallow in the extremity of my imagined martyrdom. We shared a dislike of the attitude which had brought us both up to pretend that chastity was an indispensable virtue and wished that we had grown up in the more permissive atmosphere of to-day. Joan complained that she had thought it was all her fault that her sex life with her husband had been so unsatisfactory, and I complained that, without any comparison, it was impossible to know for certain whether our sex life was normal or whether I was reaching out for the unattainable. We even discussed whether it might be a good idea for me to have a lover. Two days later, I returned home feeling far less taut. John met me at the station and he looked pleased to see me and I told him, that, while I had been away, I realised that all my agony had been through jealousy. It no longer mattered about the past, because it was past, and I was still in love with him and there was no reason why we should not make a success of this new marriage together. I warned him, however, that if I had any suspicion that he was dallying with another woman, I should not refrain from tackling, not him, but her head-on before anything developed. I was going to defend my conjugal privilege from now on without finesse. He laughed and he knew that I meant it. While I was with Joan, I had also realised how lucky we were to have this chance. Unlike so many married couples, we were both fighting on the same side for the success of our marriage: we had both had to give up so many comfortable illusions and learn to begin to face ourselves that it would be absurd to stop fighting for its survival when the battle was half won.

John was seriously looking for a job now, but he had a depressing few months. At first, he was completely honest about his alcoholism but found that this was unwise for, as I had myself found earlier when I sought work, any mention of it brought sympathy and interest but, alas, no confidence in his reliability. He was amazingly resilient in those days and refused to be cast down by his inability to find work. He attended AA meetings regularly and realised what a long way he had come; he was constantly reminded by other alcoholics of the need for patience and cheered by the evidence around him that with perseverence and integrity he could not fail to succeed in the end. I was less optimistic for I knew that we were now using for our daily requirements, besides my salary, some of the small capital that we had retained from the sale of the old house, no longer having tenants to augment my earnings. I calculated that if John did not find a job within four months we would once again have to seek an additional source of income; the house was not large enough to let a room without inconvenience and I knew that it would not help us in our present state of uncertainty on how we interrelated to have yet another person to live with us. We were learning, very slowly, a new consideration for each other, a new conception of the impossibility of ever really understanding each other and seeing the world through identical eyes, but we still needed time to recognise and interpret the warning signs to keep us away from dangerous hazards which caused emotional tension.

Although I knew the risk of carrying the parallel too far, I saw that I could learn a lot by watching David, for he seemed the most like his father, and this practice made me more aware of his reactions to me, too. I realised that, under stress, I became efficient and impatient and that this confused David so that he appeared to be stupid in his fear of upsetting me and I wondered if this was not the effect I also had on John; I had often been irritated by his apparent need to annoy me by appearing simple, thinking that he did it purposely. It was interesting and heartening, too, to watch David, who for a long time had lacked co-ordination of his limbs and was always bumping into things and falling over, suddenly gain a new sureness in movement, losing all his accustomed clumsiness; I had no doubt that this was a result of an increasing sense of security.

John had accepted the challenge to get to know himself and not hide from the frightening truths which, with the help of others, were exposed to his unwilling, tormented gaze. He began to recognise the pitfalls into which he could fall if he were unwary and now, instead of escaping into the temporary haziness of drink-induced release from the discomfort of his own nature, when the danger signals of disharmony with other people, particularly me, flickered in his mind, he cut out. At first, confused by his swings of mood, I felt hurtfully excluded when suddenly, from one moment to the next, he changed from a friendly, warm person into a cold distant stranger, but gradually I realised that if I could ignore what appeared to me to be a deliberate attempt to alienate me, and not plague him with my demands to know what had happened, why he had changed his attitude so swiftly, whether I had said something that annoyed him, he would work himself through his black isolating mood. I had thought that I had learnt to be more perceptive of how I could unwittingly upset him but I frequently blundered. I knew that his sobriety should not be, was not, dependent on my behaviour, but this seemed no reason not to help him a little by trying to avoid hurting him.

Pamela had said that I would have to change myself. I had thought that I had already changed; I no longer tried to match my will against his, nor did I try to placate him by unreasonable acquiescence to his demands, to mould myself to what I thought he wanted me to be; we both knew that we must allow each other to be what we were and not lay down a blueprint in our own minds of how the other should behave. But I recognised the need I had to look a little more critically at myself if we were to survive this new phase in our relationship. Although he had great regard for my parents, John had always been wary of my mother and her refusal to be deceived by humbug; she could not let anybody get away with affectation or inflated self-importance. We were, in my family, great debunkers, but I added a certain lighthearted cynicism which I did not intend unkindly; I thought that I was realistic. I now saw that the atmosphere of affectionate teasing in which I grew up and which took the place of outright displays of emotional attachment, had always been misunderstood by John; he only felt the criticism in the satirical remark, taking it as a sneer and not recognising the love, devoid of illusion, which lay behind our refusal to be impressed by high flown words. I relished people with sardonic wit, I enjoyed happy cynics because I had the self-confidence not to be upset by them. Michael shares my delight in lighthearted verbal battles and realises that they are not to be taken seriously. I see now that I may often have caused distress by my unintentionally hurtful jibes; I had thought I was witty. I realised that I must avoid undermining John and give up my habit of delighted exposure of what I considered pomposity.

Diana had once asked me if I needed to be such a perfectionist. I was surprised. I did not know that I was a perfectionist, but now I realised that it was true. I disliked doing anything unless I could do it well, and perhaps made John more conscious of his own shortcomings by being critical. We laughed at his ineptitude at manual tasks, as we had always laughed at my father, and I took pride in my ability to do such things as mend an electric plug when he had fumbled and joined the wrong wires. He had appeared not to mind, but perhaps he had. I recognised how unkind I was, and tried to teach myself to be less thoughtless, to encourage and not to dishearten by my comments, to be less impatient of flawed achievements, and to be grateful for the willingness and determination which John showed in tackling the most lowly household tasks whilst he was at home so that he shared the day-to-day rigours of living and bringing up a family. I saw that he was a much easier person to live with than I, with my high ideals and unrelenting standards.

We both knew that, as breadwinner, he was far more capable than I, through training admittedly, but also through a greater sense of business acumen. I liked going to work, but I did not bring in the income to support a family of six and I had no business initiative. John walked with me to the station every morning and, against my own judgement, I could not prevent a certain anxiety creeping into my conversation with him. He was trying hard to find a job and as one month succeeded the first, and then another, without success, I began to feel that he should lower his sights, that if he could not get back immediately into the professional world, he should be prepared to take some humble employment for a while to augment our income. Upon my urging, which was tinged with some reproach at his refusal to show practical appreciation of how necessary it was that he should bring in some money too, he wrote out a card, offering himself as a jobbing gardener, and had it displayed in a local shop. I was pleased: it demonstrated a spirit of humility which did not despise a lowly occupation; I did not at first realise that he had carefully outpriced himself so that nobody sought his services, and by the time I did it did not matter anyway, and the incident became a huge joke, for at the end of May, he was engaged by a local firm to practise the profession for which he had been trained. Initially his salary was low, but even then it doubled mine. By August, we had bought a second-hand car, which he insisted should be registered in my name; he wanted to own nothing until his family was established. He had paid off his debts, which amounted to less that I had thought for, once the accountants had been through his books, it was found that he was creditor as well as debtor, and his tax liability was successfully contested and agreed at a very low sum. By September, we were able to recommence paying James's school fees, and a spirit of hopefulness and success was brightening our lives. It was as if, at last, we were seeing some return on the dogged perseverance with which we had for so long tackled each new morning. In these last months before our fortunes changed, though, it was John who carried us; it was his refusal to be disheartened, and his ability to extract the greatest enjoyment from small occurrences which prevented a gloom pervading our home, for I had suffered extreme reaction after the years of holding high my banner of indestructibility. I woke up each morning laden with depression and could find no joy in the day. My job became tedious and it required extreme effort to maintain a semblance of my old enthusiasm and interest. I came home and cooked the supper and then spent the evening, lethargic, before the television screen, unable to rouse myself to any activity. I was appalled by myself and began to think that I was incapable of living without tension; now that the strain had been relieved, now that the children were content and untroubled and John growing stronger in resolve and self-assurance each day, I found life monotonous and dreary, and I dissolved into tears in face of the terrible indecision which came upon me when I had to decide what I should wear, what we should eat, whether or not to go for a walk. John was sympathetic and told me that it was understandable that I should suffer reaction after being released from all the stresses I had undergone. I had all the symptoms of acute depression, but I was convinced it would pass. I scorned his suggestion that I go to the doctor and get some anti-depressant pills. I would shame myself into activity. By August, he lost patience with me. I was on holiday, but I was not regaining any of my old energy.

'I'm fed up with you,' he said. 'I'm not at all sorry for you. If you won't go to the doctor and ask her advice and help, you have only yourself to blame.'

He was very unkind and took no notice of me. He and the boys went out in the garden and I heard them shrieking with laughter as they played some wild game.

I knew he was right and then, suddenly, I realised that he was giving me the same treatment that I had given him. He was throwing the initiative at me. He had found that kindness, and sympathy, and indulgence in my moods had not worked so he was being tough. I went to the doctor the next morning. She told me I had been a fool to think that I could cure myself, and gave me a prescription for some pills, which I took for two weeks. After that I did not need them. I was better.

I resigned from my job in October and the boys were delighted. They had not liked coming home from school to an empty house, although they had never complained or expressed in my presence a desire for a home-based mother. They were remarkably helpful in our fatherless days and reverted with delightful ease to boylike irresponsibility and evasion of duties when we were once again a complete family.

In the first weeks after his return to us, John and I both went to the group meetings which were run concurrently for the discharged hospital patients and their families respectively. At the first meeting I attended, one of the professional workers from the hospital, a wise and experienced man with an insight which frightened some of the alcoholic patients and an uncanny ability to drop into their reluctant consciousness thoughts which they preferred not to bring to the surface, brought into the discussion the concept of control. I thought this over during the following weeks: did I try to control John? Did I try to manipulate him in subtle ways, unaware myself that I was doing so? I did not believe so but resolved to guard against this possibility, and sometimes I realised that he was trying to put me in the position of being guardian of his conscience, shifting the responsibility for prudence and decision on to me so that he could be relieved of the necessity to exert self-control over his own desires and could complain that it was I who restricted him. He wanted to be restricted because he knew his own inclination to disdain caution and the danger to which this could lead, but he preferred to have it imposed on him, so I refused to make decisions for him knowing that I must leave him to make his own mistakes and not seek to guard him against himself.

At one discussion, the wife of an alcoholic said that her husband always seemed to start drinking again when he had a letter from his mother. John had made no move to communicate with his mother and I was worried that she should be excluded so completely from his life and had wondered whether I should try to engineer some rapprochement, but I was discouraged by this remark and decided not to interfere. If they wished to renew contact with each other, they were both capable of doing so without any help from me; to set my own mind at rest I wrote to her and and told her all our news but did not suggest that she should visit us.

It was on my second attendance at the group that I raised the subject of the distress I had been caused by John's admission of his infidelity; it was just after my visit north and I had, I think, already come to terms with it and begun to let it fade with all the other painful memories into the forgiven past. I had read a passage which struck home as very relevant to my condition: 'I believe in the value of suffering but not in suffering that can be avoided.'* I, too, believed in the value of suffering and I really did think that I had gained from my experiences a little more insight into myself which surely must help me to live rather less selfishly and with more generosity in my dealings with others; I hoped that I had become less mean in spirit. I understood now that I was inflicting the pain on myself by my insistence on prolonging the agony of what I chose to call John's betrayal by refusing to dismiss it from my mind as yet another result of the distorted values he had lived by for so long, his need for instant gratification of desire. At the meeting, I mentioned the confession and the great hurt it had caused me but I also said that I knew it would pass. Lightheartedly, I admitted to a temptation

* Simone Weil, *First and Last Notebooks*.

to take a lover myself and the man sitting next to me, a cheerful Cockney, stood up, bowed, and offered his services. We all laughed, my perspective swung sharply into line, and the last vestiges of my sickness of mind left me.

It was some while before I realised that sexual inadequacy or deviation is part of the syndrome of alcoholism and therefore that I need have no doubts about my own normality. Many alcoholics suffer from a fear of emasculation and a wife's scorn and contempt and distaste for a drunken husband do nothing to relieve it. Thinking that, once the drinking had ceased, my husband would be restored to me in the full vigour of masculinity, I had not shown the patience and forbearance that would have been kind when he came out of hospital. I tried to arouse his sexuality and we were both distressed by my lack of success; I learnt to avoid reading erotic novels or seeing erotic films—I thought *Women in Love* was a beautiful film but it caused me days of frantic, wilful search for distraction. One night, John asked me what it was about sex that I regarded as so ecstasy-provoking; to him it was a physical act overlaid with a fear of being possessed, of losing his identity. I realised, then, that he had never learnt to give himself and yet remain inviolate as himself, and this inhibited him in day-to-day relationships, too. What were to me the commonplace exchanges of living with other people, the give and take of life, were to him challenges against his independence which must at all times be fiercely guarded, so that to do something because somebody asked it of him could be regarded as an unacceptable subservience, not a normal courtesy; the constraint of having to allow for another's needs sometimes appeared to him as a bond of servitude, and this umanned him.

I understand that an alcoholic grows up without achieving a particular phase in his childhood maturation which is essential for his stability as an adult. There is a non-development, and therefore a distortion, in his personality caused by the failure to achieve successfully one of the stages of infancy or childhood, therefore he always operates with a deficiency which cannot be repaired, only adapted to, for he cannot retrace the period of psychological development; as a child who has lost the sight of an eye through falling on a sharp prong will never be able to relive his experience and avoid the prong and regain the sight of his eye. Only by turning to a group of similarly maladjusted people can the alcoholic maintain his stability as, in adolescence, it is the peer group which helps the youngster through those difficult years for they know emotionally how he feels in his fight to attain psychological independence from his parents. Many of us suffer from some deformity in our personalities which prevents us from behaving exactly as, ideally, we would behave in a perfect world, none of us is socialised to such an extent that we are able always to do the right thing and so mature to perfect wisdom, and we find release from our frustrations and failures by setting ourselves less impossible goals for which we can strive: money, material success, power, status. It is the excessive need for any of these, the inability to accept our own limitations, which makes for disaster and causes some of us to turn to food, sex, drugs, alcohol, to blunt the edges of our failure, but drugs and alcohol reduce the functioning of our brains and, from being able to think rationally, we also develop distorted understanding.

John may have missed out on the process of socialisation which enabled him to accept the needs of others as separate from his own needs and therefore always consciously have to adjust to those needs, but he did learn compassion for others in distress. It is I who lack this important quality and it is only because I have been made aware of this lack that I can seek now to compensate for my own inadequacy of feeling through conscious striving, at least, to act as though I do feel.

We both knew, I think, and agreed tacitly, that we are not ideally or even comfortably matched. We both needed of the other what the other was incapable of giving, but nowadays neither of us demanded the unobtainable. For both of us, there were times of loneliness, but we countered these in our separate ways usually without bitterness or much regret, and we understood that it was cruel to reproach the other for a lack of something which, perhaps, we only imagined was there in the first place. We could speak now of our difficulties and were able to guard and not barb our tongues. We had a deep understanding rooted in the knowledge that we had both had to fight our separate battles and had come through, scarred perhaps but not crippled, to a peace gained through trying to give rather than to dominate, with a family intact and unembittered. As a family, with two children in adolescence passing through all its familiar tensions, and two half-way towards it, we tried to apply our own experience in learning about ourselves to understanding their several crises, realising that for each one of them the importance they attach to sometimes seemingly trivial incidents must be respected and talked through, not dismissed or laughed at. Life is real and intense and tragic and funny and lighthearted and miserable, but above all it is a challenge. Tomorrow may bring disaster or achievement, but who cares about tomorrow?

We no longer sought confirmation of ourselves in each other. John cannot sustain my self-image with approbation, and I cannot sustain his with unquestioning, maternal-like indulgence. The cost to me of the self-discipline gained over the years is a loss of softness, of femininity, which I sometimes regret. But, in the process, I have found myself, have a very clear idea of my potential, my weaknesses, my virtues and my vices. John, too, has lost something. Instead of being able to rely on unquestioning support and sympathy in those times when he feels in need of them, he is faced with a dispassionate appraisal of his motives and a firm refusal to influence him towards a decision. The lesson of detachment was difficult to learn, but it is even more difficult to forget. When you have learnt to avoid allowing the actions of another to bring you to despair, you have also learnt to avoid trying to manipulate him by your own actions. Sometimes the result can be rather cold. But excessive emotion would be far worse for it leads to recrimination as well as dependence, a desire for revenge as well as a desire for passion. Mutual respect had to be built up first and this we had already achieved and love was always there; it is the quality of love which needed improving.

The strength and confidence that John had gained was large reward for the whole family; the trust that he had received in return was surely important to him, who had so little in the past. We both now lived honestly, by our lights; we did not play those destructive games that married couples are said to play, subtly undermining each other beneath a gloss of consideration. We had our periods of closeness, and fewer and shorter days of remoteness from each other, when it seemed that our minds were so separate that there could not be a single point of contact, that we must always go along parallel ways, within speaking distance but never reaching an intersection of understanding and empathy. When I became dismayed at this, I remembered how very much further apart those ways once were, when we could not even hear the truths that the other shouted, and only the bitterness crossed the gap between.

Chapter Ten

LAST YEAR, I had to fall back into the old routine of domesticity. I had thrown in my job of my own volition, for it had become unnecessary economically and I no longer needed it to preserve my sanity; I found the time spent in commuting ill-spent and was ready to return to the third year of my diploma course and stretch my mind a little. I had mastered the challenge of the job and it had become, for the most part, routine; I still enjoyed the company but, set against the neglect that began to show obviously in our home now that both John and I were working and the obvious enthusiasm of the boys for my retirement, I did not overvalue it. Doubtless it would boost John to be back in position as sole breadwinner but neither of us felt this fact paramount, and he was anxious that I should do what I wished for my own satisfaction.

I found it difficult to settle down but, for as long as I was immersed in my studies, I was fairly content. Once May and my examination had passed, I cast around for some occupation which would stimulate me and not allow me to sink back into the restless state of dissatisfaction with my lot to which I knew I was prone if my only function was as homemaker. I longed to do something which was socially useful and yet I could not see myself as a comforting visitor of the sick in hospital, or server of meals on wheels. To do such things would, for me, be from a sense of duty and put me in the class of do-gooders who have not the real love of people which is so necessary if they are to be done without condescension. I had no wish to play the lady bountiful. I applied to the local education authority for a temporary job in a careers office, declaring that I was willing to fulfil any function, that I wanted to experience the work and then, perhaps, apply for training. I had six weeks to spare before the boys' summer holidays started. I worked full-time for that period and John and the boys co-operated fully, scurrying around in the mornings to help me with the beds and the washing-up. On Saturdays, John vacuumed the house while I dealt with the washing and the cooking. By the end of the six weeks, I realised that I no longer wanted a full-time job because it put too much on to John. All the years of our marriage, I had resented his assumption that my proper place was at home; now that he was happy to accept that only I knew in what role I could be content, I found that I believed it to be true, at least until the boys had grown up. I noticed how they were brimful of happenings immediately they arrived home from school and appreciated an indulgent ear, how I had time to observe if something was amiss and help them to unravel their half-understood distresses. James had just completed his O-levels and had reached the age when he preferred the company of his friends to that of his family. Partly perhaps because of our family history, he was emotionally immature and needed patience and uncritical love to help him through his doubts about himself. Michael, eighteen months younger than James, had gained in maturity through his experiences, rarely being difficult to live with, and had easy relationships with all those with whom he came in contact. David, of sunny disposition, shrugged off once he was home the fact that he was usually bottom of his class but I began to fret at this one and decided he needed a different type of school; accepting himself as stupid, he proved it to himself by being mentally lazy too. I suspected that, emotionally distressed, he had cut out from learning over the past two years and had lost the habit of work. He had had two changes once he had left his preparatory school because we could not afford the fees, the first before we moved and the second after, which had not helped him, and John and I resolved that, rather than have him pitched into the rough and tumble of a large comprehensive school where his brain could so easily ossify, we must somehow afford to send him to a small school where he would get more personal attention and tuition. I knew that I could cover the fees by taking a part-time job, but I have not needed to for John has become properly valued in his work and his salary, which was already beginning to match his ability, increased when the fees became due. We have not regretted our decision for David has discovered that he is not stupid at all and has settled very happily at his new school. Andrew concerned us for a while because he was so timid, waking in the night if there was a high wind and creeping into our bed for comfort, liable to excessive fear if he lost sight of us on a country outing, avoiding the robust, spirited children at his school, but now he, too, has nearly outgrown his fears and is happy to be part of a gang.

I was determined, now that I was at home, not to allow myself to slip back into depending on John for the social side of my life or to live vicariously the achievements and disappointments of his business life; if I had, I should have become discontented for he showed little desire to spend his leisure in social activity. Before his alcoholism developed so that it seriously disrupted the whole fabric of our marriage, I had enjoyed giving the occasional party but I realised now that John disliked parties and, without the relaxation of his natural diffidence in company which alcohol had given him, had lost the easy good humour which is such an attractive part of his personality and become taciturn. Among his business colleagues, whom he met on common ground, he was natural and friendly but, in purely social surroundings, he lost spontaneity. He attended regularly two AA meetings a week and these, the occasional concert or play, and the very rare supper with old friends, satisfied him. He no longer neglected his home and, from the first day of his return to working, was punctilious in sticking to his expressed intentions, coming home each evening immediately upon leaving the office and never neglecting to telephone if he was held up. I appreciated the consideration which recognised that, if he gave me cause for alarm, it would not help us to develop the trust which was so essential in our new relationship. I was amazed how quickly I learnt trust: there were the occasional moments of panic which I tried to stifle when a situation, familiar in the past, occurred which brought flooding back in me the old feelings of uncertainty. One day I telephoned his office and was told that he was out, that he had been expected back before then and that they did not know where he was, and I felt a surge of foreboding and allowed myself to look at him suspiciously when he came in that evening. When I realised my fears were unjustified I felt ashamed and so learnt not to leap to conclusions. It took me some time to accept the fact that, when he said that he would do something, he no longer forgot; I really did not need to remind him.

In the summer holidays, perhaps because I was determined to prove to myself that I was still independent, I went away to a summer school by myself and John took the three younger boys camping while James remained at home as he had a vacation job.

It was the first time we had ever spent our holidays separately and I had never been away by myself before apart from the occasional visit to friends. Once the initial feeling of disorientation had passed, the unfamiliar sense of being among strangers who had no concern for me and with whom I had no bond, no function to fulfil, I enjoyed myself vastly, revelling in the release from all care and responsibility. I knew that I could be what or whom I liked and no one would challenge me, and yet I remained entirely myself; I even had the opportunity to indulge in light-hearted dalliance but I found that I had no desire to titillate myself with extra-marital fancies. I arrived home at the end of the week before the rest of the family, excited as a child at the thought of reunion.

I hovered on the brink of the Women's Lib movement for a short while: I believe in the breaking down of the rigid delineation between the sexes which decrees conventional role-playing and denies the possibility or desirability of unmaternal women, and I detest the double standard of sexual morality which so many men affirm by their actions, if not by their words. Naturally monogamous myself, I have no wish to impose my standards upon others. I had never attempted to judge others and was learning not to judge my own husband who, for so long, I had in some way regarded as an extension of myself, refusing to allow that all his emotions and perceptions and actions were, and must always be, his own. I went to the House of Commons to listen to the debate on the second reading of the Equal Rights Bill, but came away with the uneasy feeling that, as far as I was concerned, rights were less important than attitudes; there is a stridency about militant Women's Lib which offends me, and yet I realise the necessity for excessive zeal for a cause if attitudes are to change.

As I contemplated the increasing ease with which we lived together as a family and pondered what the future held for me and how I could best guide my own course for the maintenance of real, satisfying fulfilment, the horror and discordance of our past life seemed far away. It became difficult to remember that we were still a family at risk.

At Christmas, I asked John whether it would disturb him if I invited a few old friends in for drinks on Boxing Day: I had so enjoyed entertaining in the past. He realised that I missed these social occasions and encouraged me. He himself had reintroduced drink into the house, buying the occasional bottle of sherry and obviously enjoying being able to offer me a glass without any apparent desire to drink himself. We had wine at the table on the rare times when we entertained formally. Over Christmas, unaware that he did not drink, some of his business acquaintances had given him bottles of whisky and gin and it was pleasant to know that we could offer our guests liquor, that they were not bound by John's abstinence to abstain themselves. My Boxing Day party was enjoyable though I was aware of a certain constraint in John, who remained in the background dispensing drinks and not taking part in the uproarious game of charades which we played with the guests who remained for lunch. I knew then that our party days really were over, that though John was willing to indulge me it was putting an unnecessary barrier of difference between him and other people. I could happily abstain from drinking myself at a party and yet feel no restraint upon my conviviality but for John this was impossible.

In the New Year, the mood in the house changed. At weekends we found that we became irritable with each other but we put this down to the fact that our living-room was more restricted than it had been in our old house and that the winter weather and the resultant confinement of us all to indoors created a feeling of overcrowding, of too many limbs to trip over, too many separate hobbies to create mess, too many television programmes and too many separate tastes to be accommodated without friction. I began to look forward to Monday, when all the family dispersed, as the best day of the week.

At the end of January, one evening as I was preparing the dinner, the telephone rang.

'Hello, Mary. It's John here.'

'Yes,' I said.

'I'm in London, and I'm not sure whether I can get home for dinner before the meeting.'

It was one of his AA nights.

'All right. But won't you be hungry?'

'I've got to get to Waterloo and catch the train down. I might be able to make it.'

The indecision was unusual these days.

'Well, it's six o'clock now. You'll have to hurry.'

'Do you think I should try?'

I was increasingly bewildered.

'You must decide. What shall I tell Bob if he rings for you to pick him up?'

'I'll pick him up. I've got the car at the station and I'll pick him up from there.'

'All right. Well, we'll expect you when we see you, before or after the meeting.'

'Perhaps I can make dinner if I hurry.'

'You certainly won't if you keep talking. You'd better get to the station. Goodbye.'

I put the receiver down with a small, unwelcome suspicion in my mind. The old hesitation had been perceptible in his speech, and the indeterminacy of decision awoke fading memories. Had he been drinking?

I decided to wait and see and not predetermine my verdict. He did not come home for dinner, which scarcely surprised me for he had had very little time and, when the normal hour for his return from a meeting came, I had dismissed the suspicion from my consciousness. I was listening to a talk on the radio whilst I did the ironing. When he came in through the back door I kissed him, and then went back to him again.

'Your breath smells sweet,' I said.

I took his food from the oven and into the dining-room. He sat down to eat and I told him Bob had telephoned. Had he picked him up?

'No. I was too late. But I picked up Barry.'

'Why not Bob?' I asked. 'You must have passed his house.'

'No. I drove straight down from London.'

Then I knew for sure.

'But you said you had left the car at the station.'

He faltered.

'John, have you been . . .' No, that was the wrong approach, I must start again. 'John, I believe you have been drinking.'

He saw that I had him.

'Just one,' he said.

For a moment, I felt a flood of the old, hopeless confusion of emotion—anger, disappointment, despair. Then I gripped hard on to everything that I had learnt.

'Oh, well. I shall sleep in the spare room tonight.'

'I knew it,' he cried. 'I knew it. That there would be recriminations.'

I bit down my desire to point out that there were none and

laughed instead. The situation was so incredibly predictable, each one of the defences against discovery manifest, first the lie, then the attempt to provoke me and project the guilt by trying to put me in the wrong.

'It's not funny,' he said.

'Yes, it is,' I replied. 'And there's no point in my staying here to talk about it because you're very drunk. I'm going to bed.'

I took my night-dress from my pillow and went to the spare room. It was not until I was in bed that I felt the tension mount. I lay and wondered why he had felt the need to drink. I remembered a conversation we had had the week before when he told me that he had read an article stating that the World Health Organisation considered an alcoholic who remained dry for two years as recovered. We had, idly I thought, talked about the theory that, once his old fears and tensions are dispersed, it may be possible for the alcoholic to drink temperately. I had even said that it would make an interesting experiment which I would be prepared to risk were it not for the children. It had been a dangerous conversation but I had not appreciated then how unwisely I had spoken. Later in the week he had had several teeth removed and had been unable to eat properly all through the week-end, suffering pain and discomfort.

But what would happen now? Would he return once again to the bottle? I started to make plans of what I should do if it did progress. I felt sure that he would not relapse for long but what about the boys? It would be a terrible shock for them. I had thought that I would sleep after I had, to my own satisfaction, traced the cause of the slip, but I fidgeted in the bed, unable to relax, and jerked myself into greater wakefulness. I remembered that I had some tranquilliser pills in our bedroom, left over from the stress-ridden past, and crept in to fetch them. As I opened the door, the sweet, sickly stench of alcohol exuded through the skin hit me in the face like a recovered memory, unwelcome and undeniable. John must have drunk an enormous quantity.

The next morning, I went back into the bedroom and found John lying awake.

'I feel terrible,' he said.

'I'm not surprised. And I'm glad. Thank goodness you didn't say you are sorry.'

'I have hardly slept at all.'

I believed that. I remembered how, in the old days, after the first heavy slumber of the drink sodden, he would wake in the small hours.

We discussed why he had done it. He too had been brooding and had reached the same conclusion as I: an experiment, provoked partly by his unhappy condition of pain and discomfort and a longing to kill the pain. A physical hurt, not the old psychological inability to cope. We were both grateful that the boys had all been in bed and asleep when he came home.

The telephone rang at eight-fifteen. I had been expecting it. AA was moving in to see him through, to keep in contact and hold it until the danger was past. When he came home from the office that evening, he told me that eight people had telephoned him during the day. For myself, I was reassured. I knew that all those other alcoholics would carry him through. I really believed that the danger was over and that he had learnt, for sure, that no alcoholic can drink in moderation.

The boys did not know of his momentary lapse and there was no reason to tell them, or anybody else. The important thing was that he had gone to the AA meeting where it had immediately been admitted. When he had picked up Barry, a young man new to the group and fighting his own problem, he had thrown open the car door.

'I'm pissed as a fiddler's bitch,' John had stated.

Barry was aghast. John was one of the stalwarts of the group and everybody regarded him as a remarkable example of strength and devotion to the principles of AA, romping through the programme of sobriety—or so he had led me to understand. When they arrived at the meeting, John had tried to assume the chair because he wanted to tell them all about his feelings as he took the first drink and then followed it with another and another, but he was firmly reduced to a more lowly position. Barry told his wife when he got home that he felt terribly sorry for me; I did not know.

'You think she won't realise?' she said.

'Poor Mary,' said Barry.

'She'll cope,' replied Joanna, firmly.

I had in the past few months returned to the Al-Anon group which I had joined three years earlier, to introduce Joanna who had been referred to me by a common friend. Joanna had found the same strength in Al-Anon which I had discovered and, once back, I decided to continue attending the meetings.

John's relapse and immediate recovery really did appear to be simply a salutary experience, a practical demonstration of the correctness of the Alcoholics Anonymous assertion that no alcoholic can ever take a drink and then leave it alone.

It is widely believed that all alcoholics suffer from two common disadvantages in their sobriety: they will always be dependent personalities and they are incapable of bearing a high degree of tension. I have realised the blessing of the AA organisation in taking upon itself the strain of dependency, for a dependent relationship between two people is an unhealthy relationship and must surely end in disaster. I have been happy to hand over to AA and bear no rancour that John can speak openly at his meetings of disharmonies which he might otherwise seek to solve by using me as his scapegoat. I know that, love him as I do, I cannot bear for him the conflicts which sometimes beset him. I cannot myself experience the tensions he suffers and cannot even understand why situations which balk him should do so. I realise that he was right when he said that I enjoy tension; I do enjoy a situation which challenges me, which demands calm amidst outer turmoil: press day, the moment before a party, a demanding public occasion; I enjoy the praise gained from being a 'well-conducted young woman'. But I know now that, if I need tension to stimulate me and bring out the qualities which I enjoy exercising, I must not find it through other people. I can easily create my own tensions and I certainly do not have to involve John. If I am scared of something I have set myself to do, I can still enjoy the exertion of mind to master it, still revel in the mustering of my will and control to overcome panic, without his being concerned at all. When I sat my examinations and trembled with anxiety the night before, he was simply an amused observer, unconcerned. If I provoke a situation through my demands upon him, demands which I have now learnt he cannot meet, I am creating exactly the environment which could lead him once again into finding relief from the strain through alcohol. But I cannot and must not try to protect him from tension, for otherwise he will never learn to master it.

Two months ago, I was aware that something was troubling John. He complained of severe backache so I vaguely suggested that he go to the doctor. I asked him if he was worried about anything but he denied it. He said it would probably pass. He worked hard on painting the outside of the house at week-ends but was irritable and touchy, and I tried not to let his mood affect me. He began returning home from his office a little later than had been his custom and I wondered whether he was feeling the constraint of trying to live by the new rules he had set himself of putting the family first, before his work and personal inclinations. I could understand that for anybody who enjoyed spontaneity of action, his conformity to what he felt was desirable for us might well be irksome. He told me that he had been offered a directorship in another company and was mulling the idea over; he was tired of being in an inferior position, without the power of ultimate decision, a clerkly role. In fact, it was not and he was doing exactly the same work as he would be if he were actually boss, but it lacked the status. I was unconcerned about his status but if it worried him, then he must solve the dilemma for himself and make up his own mind whether or not he really wanted to assume the responsibility of becoming his own master with all its attendant worries. I did not try to influence him, but I became uneasy at his manner. There was a sweetness about his breath which discomfited me and yet I could not swear that it was drink which scented him: was it his after-shave lotion, or the stuff he sometimes put upon his hair? When he spoke to me, he looked straight at me and yet there was a lack of directness in his regard which was uncomfortably familiar. His conversation at the evening meal was a little less friendly than usual and several times he caused Michael, by his refusal to let a subject rest, to give me an uneasy glance. He did not criticise me and yet there was a tetchiness in him, the hint of the niggling whine of a small, tired child who wants something yet knows it will be slapped down if it tries to reach for it. Twice I challenged him but he laughed away my suspicion and I was too unsure to be firm. He told me that I was making him react because of my own uneasiness and that he knew that he was showing some of his old inconsistencies but that they were provoked by the way I looked at him which put him on the defensive. One evening, we took David and Andrew for a walk over the Downs with the dog and his remarks to me were full of provocation; when I said that I was cold and could we please walk faster he dawdled purposely pretending interest in some activity on top of the hill, and I found it less disturbing to remain silent and walk separately from him. David looked at me anxiously, and when we got home he told me that he had a horrid feeling inside him. Daddy had been like he used to be before he went to hospital. I reassured him, but knew that, if David had sensed an unnatural atmosphere, it could not be my imagination. I resolved to telephone Guy and ask him whether he thought John was drinking again, but next day John was so relaxed, so much more his normal self that I decided to wait and see. Two days passed and nothing occurred to disquiet us. Then, on Friday evening, the sweetness on John's breath was evident again and James expressed some anxiety.

'I didn't know you had noticed,' I said.

'I was trying not to,' said James.

'Well, if you've noticed and Michael has noticed and David was worried the other night, there must be something wrong,' I said.

'What are you going to do about it?' said James gruffly. 'I don't want it to get any worse.'

'I thought of telephoning Guy,' I said. 'If it goes on, I will.'

The week-end was uneventful and yet John seemed unable to settle to anything he started. On Monday night he went straight to his meeting from work and on Tuesday evening I was out. He was unusually affectionate when I came home as though he was seeking reassurance, and he told me that he was going to have dinner with his employer the next evening and make a decision about his future. That day I had a call from one of his friends, an alcoholic whom he had met in hospital and who had spent several Sundays with us in the past year.

'John's drinking again, isn't he,' said Geoffrey, without preamble.

'I'm not sure,' I said. 'I've been uneasy.'

'I'm sure,' said Geoffrey. 'I saw him at the meeting last Thursday across the room and I noticed his eyes. When I went to speak to him there was no doubt. It was on his breath.'

'Yes, I know,' I said. 'But he's been using a new dental powder and I'm not certain it isn't that. He says it is.'

'You just don't want to face it,' said Geoffrey. 'You're deceiving yourself.'

'I may be,' I said. 'But I didn't want to leap to conclusions.'

'It's obvious. And I'm worried about you and about him. It's going to get worse.'

'Maybe,' I said guardedly.

'Oh, come now, Mary, you know it's going to get worse. Stop pretending.'

'I'm not pretending,' I said. 'I told you I've been uneasy. Now I know you have noticed, too, I'm more sure.'

'Well, you know where you can get help,' he said. He was aware that I attended Al-Anon meetings.

'Yes,' I said. 'I know.' I did not wish to prolong the conversation, for Geoffrey was a pessimist and, genuine as was his concern for us, I did not find his manner helpful; he made me feel that disaster was certain to follow. I needed somebody with a more robust spirit.

'Tell John I telephoned and that I know he's drinking,' said Geoffrey. 'Get him to ring me back.'

'All right,' I said, and put down the receiver.

I dialled Guy immediately, and was relieved to find him at home.

'Guy, do you think John is drinking?'

'I'm glad you've telephoned,' said Guy. 'I've been worried about him ever since that slip in January. I don't know whether he's drinking, but his thinking is certainly awry. He's too confident, too assertive and if he's not actually drinking he's going to soon. He doesn't say anything that isn't by the book but there's no real insight and understanding in what he says. I can't fault him on his words, he talks the programme of AA but the spirit isn't there.'

'Can't you challenge him?' I said.

'I will,' said Guy. 'I've been wanting to for some time but have been uncertain how to approach him. But now I will.'

He told me that AA would rally to jerk John into an admission of the danger of his situation, and I felt relieved when I put the telephone down.

'Now it's out in the open, he'll have very little manoeuvrability,' Guy said. 'It's the emergence of the alcoholic ego, the insufferable arrogance which cannot admit it is wrong.'

'I expect that it's partly been caused by that lapse,' I said. 'He can no longer be proud of his success: the image has slipped.'

When John came home from his dinner with his boss, he was clear-eyed and direct. It seemed as though he was released from some overwhelming burden.

'I've decided what I'm going to do,' he said. 'I'm staying with the firm and my salary's going up again. I like it there and it's convenient, and I was very unsure of taking up the offer with the other people.'

'Oh, John,' I said. 'I am glad. I didn't say anything but I hoped you would. I didn't think that the other firm would be right for you.'

We sat and talked, close again, and he agreed that he had been behaving abominably. I wept a little from relief and he said he realised the strain he had put upon me, but it was all over now. I told him that Geoffrey had rung and expressed worry about him, and would he ring him back; when he had made the call, he came back and told me that it was amazing how his behaviour had been picked up, not only by me but by other people too. Geoffrey was sure he was drinking again. He did not say whether he was right.

It was David's birthday the next day and we had a happy celebration in the evening. On Friday, I had to be away all day and would not get home until late afternoon. John said that he would peel some potatoes for dinner if he was home before me. I walked in, full of my day, and he was standing at the sink. As he turned round to kiss me, my heart sank: the sweetness was on his breath again.

'You know,' he mused. 'It's amazing how these fellows rally round. Geoffrey is concerned about me and he told me that Roy was too, and they all pitch in to show their friendship.'

'Did Geoffrey ring you again to-day?' I asked.

'No. Why do you ask?'

'I wondered why you brought it up again?'

'I was just thinking how wonderful it is,' he said.

'Oh.'

On Saturday morning, he said he had to go to his office, and when he came back suggested to Andrew that they take the dog for a walk. The sweet breath was evident again. I watched them go down the road and then went out to the car. It was an office car which I did not drive. I opened the glove box but there was nothing in it but papers. I looked around for other cubby-holes but there were none, and then I saw that there was another glove box behind the driving-wheel. I opened it and found what I was searching for, a small bottle—of gin. I went back into the house and took the bottle to our bedroom and then went downstairs to await John's return. He did not come into the house when he came back from his walk but, taking a garden fork, began to dig over the front bed, near the car. I opened the front door and said:

'John, could you come in for a moment?'

He looked at me questioningly, but he came.

'Will you come upstairs?'

He followed me.

We went into the bedroom and I showed him the bottle.

'Now I am sure,' I said. 'The children have been uneasy, too: I may have to tell them.'

'You must do what you think best.'

I left him then; it was better to give him time.

He did not drink again and has not since. Once exposed, the need seemed to leave him and he only felt relief. I knew that by the time he had resolved his indecision about the job, the drink was in his blood-stream and I spoke openly to him about the advisability, perhaps, of taking plenty of sugar and liquids. I did not tell the boys and they only knew that there was no longer an uncertain atmosphere; apart from that one evening, David had not been aware of it anyway. I do not know whether John confessed at his AA meeting but he told me how glad he was I had found the bottle, and we both wondered whether he had subconsciously hoped I would find it.

We have grown closer than ever before now and those separate ways we travel are not parallel at all. They come near together sometimes, so near that they almost overlap, and when they part they are not very far away from each other. I do not know how far because I do not try to measure the distance; I know they will probably converge again and I am happy to wait.

When I began this story, I thought it would have an end. Now I know that it has no end for, from one month to the next, from one week to the next, from one day to the next, there is always something new to add, some new achievement, some new disappointment, some new despair, some new insight, some new acceptance. My husband is an alcoholic and I am content. What a paradox.